The Starlight Garden

A Thurston Hotel Novel
Book 7

MAEVE BUCHANAN

DEDICATION

To my mother, Pat Gibson,
who taught me the meaning of love.

NOTE TO READERS

Welcome to Book Seven of The Thurston Hotel Series, *The Starlight Garden*. I'm thrilled to be sharing this story with you!

In February of 2016, I was encouraged by Brenda Sinclair, the originator of the series, to join in as a co-author. Being a newcomer to the Calgary chapter of the Romance Writers of America, I'm glad that I took up the challenge! Publishing a book as part of a series is an adventure in itself, and I must say it's been a lot of fun. My co-authors have been wonderful resources for me, and I've made some great friends along the way.

Nora Fitzgerald, Jim Barnes and the other characters in this book are so real in my imagination that I feel as if they wrote their own stories through me. I believe that love always comes at the right time (even if it doesn't always seem that way). Nora and Jim's love story shows that love is possible even if you've given up on finding that special person.

The fictional town of Harmony in the Canadian Rockies reminds me of my early adulthood. I moved to Banff, Alberta the day after I turned eighteen. It was a major transition in my life, marked by freedom and independence, and what a great time I had! Living in a beautiful mountain landscape was truly a romantic dream. I met many people there that are now beloved lifelong friends. You know who you are!

Readers, I know you'll enjoy your visit to our town of Harmony. Discover the magic of the mountains. And be sure to take a walk with the one you love in the hotel gardens under the starlight…

Happy Reading!
Love, Maeve

Maeve Buchanan

www.maevebuchanan.com

ACKNOWLEDGMENTS

Thank you to the members of the Calgary Association of the Romance Writers of America for their ongoing support, guidance and friendship during the writing of this book.

A special thank you to Brenda Sinclair for encouraging me to "jump in with both feet" and be a co-author in The Thurston Hotel Series. Brenda has been a mentor, continuity editor and good friend to me throughout the creative process. Kudos to Suzanne Stengl for her meticulous work as my second continuity editor. I am grateful to those co-authors who gave me permission to use their characters in my story. Co-authors Win Day, Jan O'Hara and Sheila Seabrook were very generous with their time in regard to marketing and technical advice. Su Kopil of Earthly Charms Graphic Design did a superb job on the cover design and Ted Williams made an indispensable contribution as line editor.

No author can fail to be grateful for the support and encouragement of their family and friends as they embark on a creative project. I have been deeply blessed in that regard. To my family and many close friends, thank you for your love and faith in me.

To my readers: Thank you for reading this book! I write because of you, and I welcome your feedback and ideas. Please visit me at my website and on social media so we can get to know each other. I wish you happy reading and hope you enjoy visiting the town of Harmony!

Love,

Maeve xo

CHAPTER ONE

Nora Fitzgerald loved everything about running a New Age shop.

She especially enjoyed flipping through the wholesale catalogues, discovering some great product or book that would delight her customers. Her next monthly newsletter would feature all the new stock she was ordering and include articles on health and wellness, spiritual growth, healing modalities and of course a comprehensive listing of businesses in Harmony. She believed in helping her fellow entrepreneurs.

Jim Barnes would now be on that list.

There, it happened again. The smallest thing could take her mind to Jim Barnes. Blast! Why was that? She hardly knew the man. What made her mind keep going there? It didn't make sense.

The gentle morning rays of the July sun filled the shop with shimmering light. A tiny rainbow reflected off the prisms in the window and danced across Nora's hand. She watched it for a moment, then re-focused on her inventory and purchase planning.

Candles: order ten Love Magic, three Secret Wish and five Sweet Remembrance.

Incense: order more Nag Champa, Rainforest and Tuscany Rose.

Her mind strayed back to thoughts of Jim. The first time she'd met him had been a bit awkward. She'd arrived at the Thurston Hotel on one of her regular visits to Mrs. Arbuckle, but decided to stroll around the gardens before going inside. Walking down the path toward the gazebo, she noticed a man digging in one of the flower beds. The flower beds were gorgeous. In fact, she couldn't remember them ever looking better.

He didn't notice her, so she took the time to observe him for a few minutes. She'd heard via the Harmony grapevine that the new guy in town, Jim Barnes, was starting a garden center and now had the contract for the hotel.

The jangle of bells on the shop door jolted Nora back to the present moment. A customer was entering the shop. Nora greeted her with a smile and offered her help if she needed it.

Okay, Nora, back to work.

Jewelry: stock up on totem animal pendants. Buffalo, eagle and bear.

Essential Oils: order more patchouli, lavender and frangipani.

Henry, her Labradoodle, lay curled up at her feet, his black paw placed protectively on her shoe. He wasn't about to let her make a move without him coming along.

She glanced up at the row of glinting crystals hanging in the shop window and felt a quiet glow of satisfaction. Spirit Song Books and Gifts had become more than just a shop to the people of Harmony. It was a sanctuary. A mystical space. A haven designed for inner growth, happiness and…love.

Back to her list.

Books: send for the new meditation series and remember to restock the individual author shelves.

Tarot packs: order five Aquarian and three Rider-Waites.

Who else had such a magical purchasing list?

Her mind wandered again to her encounter with Jim at the hotel gardens. Why couldn't she forget about this guy?

* * *

The day she'd met him, he'd worn a green plaid shirt with the sleeves rolled up, faded jeans and a pair of well-worn cowboy boots. His salt and pepper hair had been slightly disheveled, curling over his sunburned neck, and he'd tied a gray bandana around his head. Handsome profile, strong back, muscular arms and hands and a very nice butt filling out his faded jeans. *Nobody could be that good-looking and not be married.*

She glanced at his left hand but didn't see a ring. So what if he didn't have a ring? Lots of married men don't wear rings if they work outdoors or with power tools. Then she remembered she'd also heard something about him having a daughter.

So he must be married.

It was disappointing to mentally check him off her already short list of available men in town. Still, she wanted to make him feel welcome. He was a business owner like herself. She moved toward him, Henry trotting beside her on his leash.

As soon as she said hello, he put his trowel down, stood up and turned toward her. His gorgeous blue eyes, set into a tanned rugged face, were magnetic. Her heart started to beat faster. They locked eyes and suddenly she realized she was staring. Not a moment too soon, he returned her greeting and patted Henry's head.

"It's gorgeous weather, isn't it?" she asked.

He nodded.

"My name's Nora Fitzgerald, and this is Henry. I run the bookstore down the street. You're Jim Barnes, aren't you? You own the new garden center?"

No wonder she hadn't seen him around before. It turned out that he'd only recently arrived in town. They discussed the upcoming Grand Opening of his store. He was a bit terse in his conversation. A man of few words. And maybe a little bit...grumpy?

Finally, an awkward silence ensued and she realized it was time to make tracks.

She felt relieved as she left him and headed into the hotel.

And she hadn't looked back, although she'd desperately wanted to.

* * *

4

Leaves were flying every which way.

Jim Barnes relished attacking an unruly hedge and shaping it to seamless perfection. It was a matter of pride to keep the Thurston Hotel grounds looking their best. Securing this long-term contract had convinced him that he'd made the right decision in moving to Harmony. Pleased with the improvements he'd made, he saw his work at the hotel as a personal thank you to the town that had made him feel so welcome.

He turned the trimmer off and watched a husband and wife wander through the gardens, admiring a flower display here and there, chatting quietly and holding hands. They seemed happy.

Would he ever be that happy again? He doubted it. The best he could do was try to forget the past and enjoy watching his daughter grow up feeling safe and secure. If Glenna could be happy, then he would be happy. It had become his mission in life. After what he'd been through with Rachelle, he couldn't imagine being with a woman again.

He restarted the trimmer and went back to work. Although he usually saved noisy jobs for times when the hotel guests were least likely to be disturbed, he'd set himself the goal of finishing the hedge because he had so much to do back at the store. After today, the hedge would be good until mid-July.

The most demanding work on a commercial property took place in the early spring. Clearing the winter debris, preparing the soil, laying sod and setting out the annuals. Another contractor had been hired to come in and do most of that before Jim arrived. Now he was bringing it all together so the hotel gardens would thrive through summer and into the fall.

Working at the hotel made a nice change from the stresses of setting up a new business. He'd left Nick, his new employee, in charge of the store for a few hours so he could come here to clean beds, pinch deadheads and do some pruning. Nick would finish putting out all the stock and plan the decorating for the Grand Opening. For refreshments, Jim had ordered a big urn of lemonade for the kids, coffee and tea for the adults and a selection of snacks and cupcakes from Whimsy, Mandy Brighton's bake shop. He'd set up a sound system for great background music, and Nick had rented a helium tank to do all the balloons. Hopefully, the Grand Opening would attract a lot of customers. He'd arrived pretty late for the gardening season. For that reason, he'd put some great sale prices on annuals, shrubs and garden decor.

He stood back and surveyed his work on the hedge with satisfaction. After finishing here, he would check the plants he'd provided for the gazebo and interior of the hotel, water those that needed it and clean away any debris before going back to the store.

Ten minutes later he was walking across the small bridge and over to the gazebo to check the hanging baskets of white petunias, grasses and trailing lobelia. The cool shade of the gazebo was refreshing after spending the last several hours in the sun. Taking a seat, he looked out onto the rest of the hotel gardens.

The memory of his first meeting with Nora Fitzgerald came to mind, as it so often did these days. At the time he'd been so busy digging up one of the flower beds at the hotel that he hadn't noticed the dark, slender figure coming down the path with a curly-haired black dog in tow.

"Hello."

Startled, he looked over his shoulder and saw a very attractive woman standing behind him. She was so beautiful that he was speechless for a moment. She was wearing a long dress of pale cream which fitted her perfectly, showing off the contours of her body. Well-proportioned breasts, slender waist, generous hips. Her long dark hair tumbled over her shoulders in easy waves and her large blue-green eyes had otherworldly depths. He guessed she was in her thirties. Suddenly he realized he was staring. He stood up.

"Um, Hello. Nice day." He patted the dog on the head while noticing her smile went all the way up to her eyes. It was a warm and genuine smile that instantly captivated him.

"It's gorgeous weather, isn't it?" She was carrying a basket with a cloth over it. He nodded.

"My name's Nora Fitzgerald. And this is Henry." She reached down and scratched behind Henry's ear. "I run the bookstore down the street. You're Jim Barnes, aren't you? You own the new garden center?"

He nodded again. "News travels fast here."

Nora laughed. "Yes, I'm afraid that we don't have many secrets in Harmony, and if we do we don't keep them long! So you're having a Grand Opening?"

The kindness of her expression and the tiny crow's feet on either side of her eyes made her even more appealing.

"Yep, pulling out all the stops. It's in two weeks."

Nora beamed. "Well, count on me attending, I have a long list of things I need for my garden."

Again, he found himself at a loss for words.

"Well, I'd better be going. I'm on my way over to the hotel to visit Mrs. Arbuckle. Have you met her? She's one of my best customers."

"Not yet."

Nora held out her hand and he shook it briefly.

"Nice meeting you, Jim. If I don't see you before next weekend, I'll see you at the Opening."

And with one more flash of her smile she'd left, moving away from him toward the hotel. He'd watched intently as she went, hoping she'd turn and look at him again.

CHAPTER TWO

"Nora! I'm so glad to see you, dear!" Mrs. Arbuckle said as she opened the door of her suite and stood to one side to allow Nora and Henry to enter. A small white dog jumped down from the sofa and ran up to Henry. The two dogs touched noses, tails wagging.

"Hello, Betty Jo!" Nora reached down and rubbed the smaller dog's ears. "I brought you that new book you wanted, Mrs. A. I hope you like it."

"I always love the books you bring me, dear. Now how about a nice cup of tea?"

Nora settled comfortably in an overstuffed chair by the fireplace as Mrs. Arbuckle phoned down for room service. She always felt very much at home when visiting Mrs. A.

"Now, tell me all the news, Nora." Mrs. Arbuckle turned toward her guest with an expectant look as Betty Jo jumped back up on her lap.

Nora smiled. "News from here or…there?" she asked mischievously. She was referring to Mrs. Arbuckle's late husband who now resided in the spirit world.

Mrs. Arbuckle knew that Nora was not only psychic but had significant gifts as a medium. She was one of the few people who understood and respected Mrs. Arbuckle's connection to her dear departed Walter.

Mrs. Arbuckle leaned towards Nora and patted her hand.

"There, of course! Has my Walter been behaving himself around town?"

Nora nodded. "It seems so. But he doesn't tell me everything, you know!"

Mrs. Arbuckle chuckled. "He's always up to something! What's the latest?"

Nora clasped her hands behind her head. "Well, apparently we're going to have a great summer weather-wise. He's advising me to plant more annuals."

"He always was a great one for predicting weather, even when he was still with us in the flesh."

Nora smiled. "I also think he's been showing my dog the best spots in the yard to bury the socks and underwear that Henry steals from the laundry. I could do without that, frankly!" she said, laughing.

Mrs. Arbuckle shook a be-ringed finger at Nora's dog. "Oh Henry! You bad boy! You need to behave!"

Betty Jo jumped down and began chasing Henry around the room, her tail wagging madly. It was a miracle that the two dogs managed to play without knocking anything over.

A soft knock sounded on the door and Poppy, the hotel maid, arrived, carrying a large silver tea tray into the room.

"Just put it here, Poppy dear." Mrs. Arbuckle pointed to the coffee table in front of the sofa. Poppy set the tray down carefully, nodded to Nora, and was gone.

The delicate English flowered tea set was Mrs. Arbuckle's own, kept specially for her in the hotel kitchen. Accompanying the well-steeped and fragrant Darjeeling tea was a selection of tiny sandwiches and tea cakes. White linen napkins, milk and sugar were laid out with the gleaming silverware. Tea time was a noteworthy occasion in Mrs. Arbuckle's world.

Mrs. Arbuckle graciously poured tea into Nora's cup, then offered the milk pitcher. Nora added some milk to her tea, stirred it and picked up a cress and cream cheese sandwich.

Mrs. Arbuckle reached for an egg salad.

"I hear there's a new store in town. Some kind of garden center?"

Nora nodded.

"That's right, there's a Grand Opening in a couple of weeks. I talked to the owner. He's got the contract for the hotel gardens."

Mrs. Arbuckle raised an eyebrow.

"A new man in town? Tell all, dear! Is he single or wed?"

"Married, I'm thinking. He has a daughter." Nora was painfully aware she was blushing.

"Really…how interesting." Mrs. Arbuckle may have noticed the blush but didn't comment on it. "Good-looking?"

"I guess…" Nora didn't want to reveal what she really thought. "A little older than me. Kind of brusque.

His name's Jim Barnes." Nora nibbled the last of her sandwich and took another.

"Brusque? I can't imagine anyone being brusque with you, my dear. As for the gardens, I hadn't noticed. I haven't been out yet this week for my stroll around the grounds. So, I'll make sure I go to that Grand Opening to meet this brusque and mysterious Jim Barnes."

Nora was anxious to change the topic, although she couldn't say why. Luckily, Mrs. A did it for her.

"What else have you heard from my Walter?"

"Well, he was telling me about Brock and Riley getting ready for their wedding. It should be quite a bash!"

Mrs. Arbuckle sipped her tea and reached down to pet Henry, who had noticed there were sandwiches on the table. He fixed Mrs. Arbuckle with big sad dog eyes.

"Poor Henry. Poor starving dog!" Mrs. Arbuckle patted his head. "You'd think your Mama never fed you!" She snuck a little piece of her sandwich to Henry. Instantly Betty Jo was in on the action and got her own piece of sandwich. Both dogs lay down on the carpet and swiveled their heads back and forth between the two women, watching them eat.

"Now you've done it!" Nora groaned. "We're going to be under close scrutiny until I leave."

She took a long sip of her tea.

"I'm going to have coffee with Riley this week," Nora continued. "She's excited, but I know her mother's driving her up the wall."

Mrs. Arbuckle grimaced. "Ah, Lilith. She's a caution."

"Well, it doesn't help that she keeps telling Riley about the hazards of marriage. Why doesn't she let Riley alone so she can enjoy anticipating the event?"

"'Twas ever so with mothers, dear. The maternal instinct to protect the young is something fierce. The trouble is, we older women forget that you younger women have your own path, your own history and your own wisdom."

"Thank you, but I always appreciate your wise words, Mrs. A."

"Someday it will be your turn, Nora. You'll be planning your own wedding. In fact, I bet Walter has the perfect man in mind for you. He loves to make matches."

"Really? I can't think who that would be." Nora blushed for the second time and shook her head. "There's a very limited pool of eligible guys in Harmony."

"Things have a way of working out. You know that, Nora. Trust your intuition!"

Nora smiled warmly at the older woman. "What would I do without you and Walter, now that my parents are so far away? It really helps to have your friendship."

"And your friendship means the world to us, dear." She refilled Nora's cup.

* * *

A week later, Jim Barnes was in his kitchen, adding the finishing touches to a ham sandwich. Cutting it in four pieces, he put it on a plate and placed it on the kitchen table.

"Glenna, here's your lunch, honey."

"Dad, where's my hoodie?" Glenna was looking around the kitchen.

"Right on the sofa where you left it last night." Glenna ran into the living room and pulled her blue hoodie off the back of the sofa.

Jim went to the fridge, poured a glass of milk and placed it next to the sandwich. Glenna sat down and took a few bites.

"Dad! I'm going over to the school this afternoon to meet Dolly Smythe and I need a note so I can join the summer soccer league!"

Jim leaned back against the counter, crossed his arms and raised his eyebrows. "Summer soccer league?"

Glenna sipped her milk. "It's at the school grounds. Dolly Smythe told me about it. I can join, right?"

Her father nodded approvingly. "I don't see why not. Who's coaching?"

"The principal and some of the teachers. And Mr. Farraday is helping too."

Jim pulled some paper out of the kitchen drawer, hastily scribbled a note and handed it to Glenna. "Put this in your hoodie pocket. Okay, Sprout?" He poured himself a cup of coffee and sat down across from her. "Let them know I'd be glad to coach if they ever need me."

"Yes, Dad." Glenna beamed as she finished her lunch.

* * *

Glenna had to walk briskly, even though it was only three blocks to the school grounds. She didn't want to be late.

In recent days she'd noticed that Dad seemed happier. He'd been so sad when they first came to Harmony, but once he'd found a house for them and started working on his new business, she'd noticed a change. She knew things were getting better when he started whistling and calling her "Sprout" again.

Being the new kid in town at the start of the summer holidays wasn't easy. She was slowly getting to know a few people around town. She'd met Reba and Dolly Smythe last week in the park. They were cool. And now she would meet more kids at soccer practice.

Glenna loved soccer and was proud of her skills. She knew her dad would come to every game, no matter what. He had often helped coach her team in Calgary. She was grateful for this as she noticed that not all parents showed up regularly. She felt sorry for those kids. She only had Dad but she knew she could always count on him.

Glenna gave a few little skips. She still worried about fitting in here, but things seemed to be getting better lately. She even had a new adult friend. That was awesome.

She'd met Nora Fitzgerald just two days ago. Walking by Spirit Song Books and Gifts on Main Street, she had seen a beautiful little embroidered bag in the window.

She stepped inside the shop and immediately felt she was in a wonderful place, with interesting stuff to look at, peaceful music playing, and the spicy perfumed smell of burning incense creating a sense of mystery and adventure. Nick Danyluk, who also worked at her father's garden center, was putting candles on one of the shelves.

"Hello!" A cheery female voice called out from the back of the store. Nick looked up, waved briefly at Glenna and then returned to his task. Glenna was still looking at Nick when a nice-looking lady walked up to her, smiling.

"Hi, I'm Nora. Can I help you with something or are you just browsing?" The lady's eyes were warm and friendly.

"Just browsing, I guess." Glenna smiled back at the woman. "I'm new in town. My name's Glenna Barnes."

"Pleased to meet you, Glenna, and welcome to Harmony! I met your Dad last week over at the hotel. Feel free to ask me about anything in the store - I'll leave you to explore."

Glenna moved around the store, picking up various items to inspect them. Eventually she came back to the counter where the lady was writing in a book.

"I really like that bag in the window. The one with the embroidery," Glenna said, pointing. Nora went over to the window, picked up the bag, brought it back and placed it in Glenna's hand.

"This bag comes all the way from India," Nora explained. "Native women in a small town make their living out of sewing these bags, and they are paid a fair wage for them. I make sure I only buy fair trade items that benefit communities. Isn't it lovely? Those ladies are so talented."

"Yes, they are. This bag is pretty. It would be a good place to keep treasures." Glenna turned the bag over in her hands. It was covered in flower patterns and little elephants, with a long strap that could be worn over the shoulder or tucked into the bag. The flap had a little golden tassel hanging from it.

Nora nodded.

"Do you have special treasures at home, Glenna? I know that I do. I have a little wooden box that I keep mine in."

"I have some jewelry my grandma gave me, and some cards from people, and pictures of my family."

"Those are excellent treasures. I also have pictures of my family, and some of my friends." Nora reached over to a nearby shelf and picked up a small round pale pink stone.

"Do you know what this is?"

Glenna shook her head.

She placed the stone in Glenna's hand. "It's called pink quartz. These stones are full of positive energy and are a special treasure that you can give to a close friend or loved one."

Glenna rubbed the smooth surface with her thumb. Inside the stone were spidery webs of white and pink. She loved it.

"This is so neat!" She looked up at Nora and smiled.

"You keep it, Glenna," Nora answered. "I hope you will be a new friend and think of me when you look at it."

"I'd like to be your friend!" Glenna was thrilled. This grown-up lady wanted to be her friend! "Thank you so much, Nora. I guess I better go," Glenna said regretfully, then looked up at Nora again with a hopeful expression.

"Would it be okay if I came in again soon? I have to go home right now but I'd like to see more."

"I'll tell you what I tell all my new friends, Glenna. You are welcome anytime."

Glenna started to hand Nora the embroidered bag but Nora pushed it back.

"Keep the bag to store your treasures in, Glenna. It will be our secret."

Glenna was beaming.

"I'm going to put my pink quartz and all my other treasures in it. Thank you so much, Nora!"

"No problem, friend. I'll look forward to seeing you next time you come in."

Glenna remembered all this as she walked to the school. Yes, she was glad that her dad had decided to move here. She ran onto the soccer field where Dolly was waiting for her.

CHAPTER THREE

Nick Danyluk unpacked the last of the stock. Nora had recently received a new order and there was a lot of shelving to do. After finishing here, he had to run over to Jim's Yard and Garden Center to begin decorating for the Grand Opening.

Nick felt lucky to have found not one, but two part-time jobs in Harmony. He'd only been in town for a few months, after all. First, he'd found a place to live. He'd met his new roommate, Gill, one night at The Wobbly Dog. Gill didn't make a lot of money working at the Thurston Hotel and had been looking for someone to share the rent. The two had ordered a pitcher of beer and hit if off right away. So that worked out perfectly. He'd scored the Yard and Garden Center job last week.

Nick Danyluk, he thought to himself, *you may yet have a future in this town.*

He unwrapped the incense. He didn't get why people loved the stuff. It made his nose itch. Maybe he had an allergy. He finished putting out the rest of the boxes as quickly as possible and moved on to the tarot decks.

This New Age stuff was a mystery to him, but he really liked his new boss. Nora had hired him soon after he arrived in town. She set out her expectations clearly, and had paid him promptly after his first week. For an older woman, he thought she was pretty hot. Way, way too old for him, though. He already had his eye on someone in town. Gill had introduced him to Angelina Fernandez one day when he stopped at the hotel to drop off Gill's keys. Angelina had a face like…an angel. And a gorgeous body. Her name suited her perfectly. He knew he had to figure out a way to ask her out. Maybe Gill could help.

* * *

Jim Barnes was looking over the greenhouse plants when he felt a small pair of arms go around his waist.

"Hi, Dad!"

He turned around and scooped Glenna up for a hug and a kiss.

"How's my girl? How was soccer?"

"Great! The coaches are awesome. Dad, can I get a new outfit for the Grand Opening?"

Jim hated to refuse his daughter anything. "We'll see, honey. Things are kind of tight until we get this business going. Remember I explained that to you?"

Glenna sighed. She picked up a decorative glass sphere from a table nearby and rolled it around in her fingers. "Yes, I know. Tighten our belts."

"That's right. Listen, let's look at your clothes tonight after dinner and figure out the perfect outfit. Maybe we can get some new accessories. What do you say?"

Glenna smiled at him. "Ok." She put the glass sphere down and was silent for a few moments.

"Dad?"

"Yes?"

"Where's Nick from?"

"Calgary, I think. Why do you ask?" Jim brushed the hair from her forehead.

"No reason." Glenna fiddled with some decorative garden stakes. "How old is he?"

"Um, about twenty-four." Jim suddenly woke up to his daughter's interest. "Do you like him, Sprout?"

"I guess. Did you know he was working at Nora's store?"

"I did, yes." Jim thought it was time to change the subject. "Soccer was over awhile ago, wasn't it? Where have you been?"

"I stopped at Nora's store after soccer." Glenna said.

Jim frowned. "Don't be bothering her now, Glenna."

"But Dad, the first time I went to her store, she said I was always welcome."

"Well, just be aware if she's busy, okay?" Jim didn't know how he felt about his daughter getting so close to Nora. He was aware that he seemed to be thinking about Nora Fitzgerald a lot lately. He didn't want Glenna getting too attached to her unless he could monitor it.

* * *

Later, at home, Jim started dinner while Glenna sat in the living room reading. He had learned to cook and take care of a house long before he met Rachelle, his crazy ex-wife.

Good thing, since he was now a single parent. Raising a child alone wasn't easy, but it was definitely easier than raising a child with Rachelle. He was grateful that Glenna had been so young when Rachelle left them, but it didn't stop his daughter from asking all kinds of awkward questions. He didn't want Glenna to know where Rachelle was, so he'd simply told her that her mother had gone away on a long trip and he didn't know if she would be back. As Glenna got older, her questions got harder and harder to answer. One of these days he would need to tell her the truth, but he had no idea how he was going to do that. He'd spent a lot of sleepless nights worrying about it.

He drained the spaghetti and placed it in a bowl, stirred in some butter, then poured in his homemade tomato sauce. He shredded some fresh parmesan on top and tore up some basil leaves for garnish.

"Set the table please, honey."

Glenna put away her book and set two places. Jim poured a glass of milk for Glenna and a glass of water for himself. He placed the pasta on the table along with a green salad he had prepared earlier.

"There you go, sweetie. Dig in!"

Glenna twirled her pasta around her fork and took a big bite.

"It's yummy, Dad!"

"Thanks, Sprout. Cookies for dessert?"

"Yes, please!"

He watched Glenna eating. What a beautiful daughter he had. How a human train-wreck like Rachelle had produced such a sweet child, he'd never know. Glenna had been a good baby, a lively toddler and a delight through her early school years. Oh, there were the usual tantrums and childhood crises, but overall he was lucky to have such a great kid who cared about other people. She got good grades in school and was a heck of a soccer player. He was proud of her.

"More milk?"

"Yes, please."

Jim filled her glass.

"Save some for dunking cookies," he reminded her.

After Glenna was born, Rachelle had started behaving strangely and disappearing for days at a time. She had shown absolutely no interest in her baby. He had been totally confused by this and soon discovered where Rachelle was going and what she was doing. It was then he realized that he had no idea who he had married.

Rachelle had been drinking and drugging before and during their marriage. It was a miracle that Glenna had been born without any side effects from her mother's self-abuse. Jim spent the next four years caring for their baby and dragging Rachelle out of bars and shooting galleries. He had no other choice. For richer or for poorer, in sickness and in health. He took his marriage vows seriously. He had tried to make it work and hoped that someday Rachelle would seek help for her addictions.

Then Rachelle disappeared. She'd left before, but always came home a couple of days after a binge. On the fourth day, he reported his wife missing. Two weeks later, an RCMP officer in Calgary had phoned to inform him that his wife had been arrested. Drug dealing, possession of an unregistered firearm, and solicitation. Firearm? Solicitation? It was worse than he thought.

He'd attended all the court dates, and a combination of sadness, anger, guilt and relief flooded over him when Rachelle was sentenced to eight years' hard time with no possibility of parole. He was concerned for her, but he also felt free of anxiety for the first time since Glenna's birth. He hoped this would be the turnaround for her. It was Rachelle who filed for divorce after her first year in jail. He was saddened by this, but didn't fight it. He turned all his attention to caring and providing for his daughter.

He got up and put some cookies on a plate and set them on the table. Glenna immediately dunked one in her milk.

Yes, now he remembered. Glenna had been four when Rachelle was arrested.

Jim's heart suddenly plummeted.

Eight years ago. That meant Rachelle was due to be released this year! What if she came to Harmony? *Oh God.*

He'd gone to a lot of trouble to prevent Rachelle from finding out where they were. He told friends and family to keep his new location to themselves. But people like Rachelle had ways of finding out things. Should he prepare Glenna? Or just hope for the best?

He would have to think this through. He stood up and started clearing the dishes from the table.

CHAPTER FOUR

Nora pushed open the front door of Whimsy and quickly spotted Riley Hamilton sitting at one of the tables by the window.

"Hey, girlfriend!" Riley gestured toward the seat across from her. "I've already got my coffee, what can I get you?"

Nora leaned over and gave her friend a peck on the cheek before taking her seat. She had known Riley for many years, and was very fond of her. Riley had grown up to be a very beautiful woman, and here she was, getting married. Time sure did fly.

"Thanks, Riley. A peppermint tea would be great."

Her friend waved at Kelsey Archer, who was tidying up behind the counter.

"Could we get a peppermint tea please, Kelsey?"

Kelsey waved back and in a few minutes brought the tea to Nora.

Nora looked up. "Thanks, Kelsey. How are you today?"

"Just fine, thanks. Cupcake, anyone?"

Riley shook her head. "Not for me, thanks! I've got a wedding dress to fit into. Besides, if my mother spotted me eating a cupcake, I'd be hearing about it for the next year!"

Nora laughed. "I'm fine, too, but thanks."

"Ok…let me know if you need anything." Kelsey picked up an empty cup off a nearby table and went back behind the counter.

Nora smiled at Riley. "So, how is the planning coming along?"

Riley groaned. "Nora, if I'd known how much work it is to put on a wedding, I think I would have asked Brock to elope! It's never-ending! And everyone, but everyone, has an opinion on every tiny thing. Especially my mother."

Nora wiped a stray drop off her cup with a napkin. "How is your mother? And your dad?"

"Oh, they're fine. I'm the one having the nervous breakdown!" Riley grimaced and rolled her eyes.

"Never mind." Nora patted Riley's hand. "Let's have fun today figuring out what you want to do for guest favors at the wedding dinner."

Riley pulled a crumpled piece of paper out of her leather purse. "Well, I've decided I'd like little white organza bags tied with red ribbon to match the wedding theme. I thought I'd leave one above each plate on the table. What do you suggest I put in them?"

Nora thought for a moment and pulled a small notepad and pen out of her coat pocket. "I can order the bags and ribbon today. Would this size do?" Nora showed the size of the bags using her hands. "They are small but hold a lot of small items."

Riley nodded approvingly.

"I'm first going to suggest you put in some tiny crystals that I have in the shape of snowflakes." Nora wrote on her notepad.

"Perfect!" Riley tapped her fingers on the table. "What about something heart-shaped?"

Nora thought it over. "I have these little mini magnets that are red glass hearts. Would that work?"

"Can I see them first?"

"No problem, stop by the shop later and I will pull out everything for you to see. We may have other options."

"Okay." Riley bit her bottom lip. "How about stars? I love stars."

"I have crystal stars that are the same size as the snowflakes." Nora said.

"Good, that will work. Maybe two stars and two snowflakes per bag. Now for something red, besides the magnets."

"I have tiny red tea lights, which I can wrap individually in silver cellophane paper."

Riley nodded. "Excellent."

Nora wrote each item carefully on her notepad. "Also, I'd like to suggest little cards - I have some great mini cards with love quotes on them. We could have them printed with your names on the reverse side."

Riley's face broke into a big grin. "That would be great! I love your suggestions. I think that's will cover it, don't you?"

Nora nodded. "Agreed. Besides, I have to get back to work in a few minutes. You can look around the shop later for more ideas. Let's finish our drinks. I'll call you on your cell later when I have everything put together."

"You're awesome. This is one more thing I can check off my list!"

Nora cupped her hands around her tea and met Riley's eyes. "You must be so excited."

Riley thought for a moment. "Excited, yes. Of course I'm thrilled to think of spending my life with Brock, but truthfully, the reality of the wedding hasn't quite sunk in yet. Too much to do. It's sort of like when you go on a trip…you plan and plan, but you don't really feel like it's happening until the plane takes off."

"That makes sense."

"Speaking of weddings," Riley continued, "I'm surprised no one has snatched you up yet, Nora! You've always been so gorgeous, and now you're a successful business woman. What are all the men thinking, with a gem like you on the market?"

"Thanks, but you know how it goes. I've dated a few nice guys over the years, but no one that seemed like…the one. Besides, Harmony has a limited number of bachelors who are the right age. I'm thirty-eight, after all. I'm happy enough with things as they are."

Nora didn't tell Riley that she had been thinking non-stop of Jim Barnes ever since she met him.

"What about Brock's uncle Reg? He's pretty cute...for an older guy. I could fix you up."

Nora smiled and shook her head. "No, thank you! I stopped letting people fix me up long ago. But you are a sweetheart to ask. Don't worry about me, Riley. I'll probably end up as one of those interesting old maids that travels the globe. I'm not really lonely. Besides, I've got Henry to keep me company."

Riley raised an eyebrow. "Pets are great, but no substitute for a man's arms around you."

Nora knew this was true. She was a passionate soul. Her intuition told her that love would come her way at the right time. But she often wondered if she should be more proactive in the process. Would she ever find someone who loved her like Brock loved Riley? It seemed a long, long time since she had been kissed or held. She missed the thrill of being in love, of doing things with someone special. She sometimes wished she had settled for one of the men she had dated, but then none of them had really been a good fit. Had she made the mistake of being too picky? She sipped the last of her tea. "Well, I guess if I'm meant to be with someone, I will be. Lord knows I have enough to do running Spirit Song."

"Never mind, Nora. This is going to be a big wedding - I bet you'll meet someone!"

"Maybe." Nora smiled warmly at her young friend.

CHAPTER FIVE

Jim stood on his back porch with his coffee in hand, looking out at the yard. Seven a.m. and the Saturday of the Grand Opening had dawned clear and sunny. That was a relief.

It was the case of the shoemaker's children going barefoot. He had spent so much time starting his new business and fulfilling the Thurston Hotel garden contract that he hadn't had a chance to work on landscaping his own home.

He sighed. Once he and Glenna got through the event today, they could sit down and start planning the landscaping for their house. He'd been surprised at Glenna's natural talent for landscape design which he supposed she'd inherited from him. He would offer Nick some extra hours to help improve things around the home front.

His mind went back to Glenna. If she inherited her green thumb and designer's mind from him, what had she inherited from her mother? He dreaded to think. Did Rachelle have any redeeming qualities? He couldn't think of a single one. Glenna must have some of her mother's gene pool. Would Glenna's teenage years bring out negative traits that she shared with Rachelle?

Okay, okay. Don't borrow trouble. You've got a fantastic girl and Rachelle is out of the picture for good. She couldn't care less about her daughter, so it's unlikely she will turn up. He'd better go in and get dressed, then head to the store. Nick was already there, getting everything ready.

He picked out a blue shirt and a clean pair of jeans and laid them on the bed. He'd polished his boots last night. Looking in the mirror in the bathroom, he took stock. Not bad for a forty-two-year-old guy. A lot of outdoor living had given him quite a tan and a few extra lines. He knew he looked his age, but he wasn't unattractive. Maybe it wasn't too late to meet someone. But he had so much baggage. It wouldn't be fair to put that on a woman, and even if he liked her a lot, she would have to be a very strong woman to handle it.

Nora Fitzgerald. Smart, beautiful and kind to his daughter. How would it be to date her? Could she handle his history? He couldn't stop thinking about her, even though he tried to. Was it fair to even try to get to know her better?

Half an hour later, Jim pulled his truck into the parking lot in front of the garden centre. He and Glenna jumped out. Nick stood on a ladder, fastening the final bouquet of balloons to the roof.

"Hi, Nick!" Glenna yelled, heading into the building. "Dad, I'm going to set up some tables for Mandy."

"Hey, Mr. B! Ready for the big opening?" Nick asked as he climbed down the ladder. "I've pretty much finished up. Mandy's coming over in a few minutes with the drinks and cupcakes."

Jim stood, hands on hips, looking up at the decorations. "Good job, Nick. Did you get all the specials marked?"

"Marked and ready. Do you want those pink geraniums in the front display?"

"Go ahead. Use the tiered shelves for them. And don't forget to make sure the selection trays are ready for people to pick up at the front as well." Jim headed for the greenhouse to do a final check on stock.

He bit his lip. What if no one showed up? He was counting on this event to increase revenue. The contract at the Thurston helped, but it wasn't enough to keep him and Glenna going. He had great plants, as well as garden ornaments, tools, seeds and everything else any gardener could need. From the yards he'd seen around town, lots of keen gardeners lived in Harmony.

The Grand Opening was scheduled for nine o'clock. By ten o'clock the store was swarming with customers. Glenna was busy working the refreshments table with Mandy, and Nick was working the till, answering questions and directing customers to different areas of the store. People came up to congratulate Jim and those who hadn't met him yet welcomed him to town.

By two o'clock, he knew everything was going to be fine. He had sold enough to cover his initial costs, and landed a few solid contracts for landscaping and yard work.

But he still hadn't seen Nora. Between chatting with customers, he'd scanned the crowd, but she was nowhere. Maybe she wasn't coming. Why was it so important to him that she be here?

Then, he saw her. Over by the geranium display, talking to a petite older woman.

He headed over. As he got closer, his pulse quickened and he started to sweat. What was he? A teenager trying to ask a girl to the prom? Get a grip!

Nora and her companion looked up as he approached, big smiles on their faces.

"Hi, Jim! What a great opening! I'm starting to stock up." Nora pointed to her tray which already contained some yellow pansies, pink geraniums and a variety of fresh herbs.

"Jim, I'd like to introduce my friend. Mrs. Arbuckle, Jim Barnes."

Mrs. Arbuckle extended her hand and Jim shook it gently.

"Very pleased to meet you, Mrs. Arbuckle."

"As I am to meet you, young man. This is an impressive event."

"Thank you. Can I offer you ladies a drink? Tea, coffee, lemonade?"

"Lemonade for me please, dear. Nora?"

Nora nodded. "Thanks, Jim, I'd like the same."

* * *

As Jim walked to the refreshments table, Mrs. Arbuckle caught Nora watching him.

"A very good-looking young man, Nora. And well-mannered. Are you sure he's married?"

Nora did not have time to answer before Jim returned with their drinks.

"Mrs. Arbuckle lives in the hotel," Nora explained.

"I hope I'll see you there." Mrs. Arbuckle sipped her lemonade. "I understand you're the new gardener. I try to take a turn around the gardens when I have time. I must say you've done a fine job so far."

"Thank you, Mrs. Arbuckle. I do my best. Please excuse me ladies; I have to help with some of the orders."

"Certainly, dear. Nice to meet you."

"Bye, Jim," said Nora. "Hope you do well with the sales."

He was already moving away from them. Nora felt somewhat deflated as she watched him go.

"Cheer up, dear. You'll see him again."

Nora turned and looked at Mrs. A. "What? Oh…yes. Well, I'd better finish picking out my flowers."

Mrs. Arbuckle pointed out to the street.

"Here's my car from the hotel. Do enjoy yourself, Nora. Tea later?"

"I'd love to."

"See you then, dear."

Mrs. Arbuckle left her and walked to the car. Gill held the door open for her.

Nora waved then turned back toward the greenhouse. She picked out some sweet william and a few begonias for the shady spots near her porch.

Suddenly Jim was back, standing beside her. "Finding everything you wanted?"

"Yes…still looking. The plants are all so healthy and beautiful." Nora caught her breath. He was close, very close. He reached across in front of her to pick up a small pot of violas.

"This might go well with the pansies," he offered, looking directly into her eyes as he handed it to her. Her heart raced. For a moment both were silent, simply looking at each other.

"Nora…" Jim began.

"You found Nora!" Glenna squeaked as she ran up to them. "Nora, do you want a cupcake? We have maple cupcakes. They are sooo delicious!"

"I'd love one, Glenna." Glenna grabbed Nora's hand and started pulling her toward the refreshments table. Nora cast a glance back at Jim, who shrugged and smiled.

If he'd intended to say something, he'd changed his mind.

* * *

In the Thomas Lounge at the hotel, two old friends were sharing a drink.

Madeline Arbuckle sipped her vodka on the rocks. "Well, Emily dear, it's been quite a week. Did you manage to get to the Grand Opening of the new Yard and Garden Center today?"

Emily Jamieson wrapped her fingers around her glass of Baileys. "I did. That Jim Barnes that owns the place is quite nice, not to mention good-looking. I noticed he was talking to you and Nora."

Maddie smiled. "Yes, he was. I really like that young man. He's well-mannered. There's a twelve-year-old daughter, you know. I haven't heard anything about his wife, though. If it turns out that he's divorced or a widower, I was thinking he'd be a good match for our Nora."

Emily nodded in agreement. "It's about time Nora settled down. She's such a lovely girl."

Maddie swirled the ice cubes in her almost empty glass. "Emily, I've been thinking."

"Maddie, you shouldn't do that. You tend to meddle, you know."

Her friend shook her head. "Me? I don't meddle. You do."

"I certainly do not. I know how to mind my own business."

"Emily dear, you obviously weren't minding your business when you tried to stop your daughter from marrying her boyfriend."

Emily frowned. "I was protecting her."

"Of course you were. You were thinking of what was best for her."

"I didn't want her to have to get married. Not like I did." Emily clamped her mouth shut. "Forget I said that."

"Why, did Mary *have to* get married?"

Emily glanced around and then leaned in. "I don't know. I really don't know if she was—" she lowered her voice to a whisper - "*pregnant.*"

Maddie nodded sympathetically.

"At any rate, I told her not to come crawling back when she needed money," Emily continued, staring into her crystal glass. She shook her head. "I should never have said that. I didn't really mean it."

After a moment of silence, Maddie resumed her questioning.

"What was his name?"

"Whose name?"

"Mary's boyfriend's name."

Emily's brow creased. "I can't remember! It was a lifetime ago."

Maddie pressed on. "Try to remember."

"Patrick? No, not Patrick. Although maybe that was his last name. Kirk? Kirby? I can't remember. I doubt she would have stuck with him anyway. They were so young. Can we talk about something else?"

Maddie nodded. "Of course, dear. I'm sure you'll remember in time. Now, let's talk about how we can find out about Jim Barnes' marital status. If he's divorced or widowed, maybe we can get him and Nora together."

They waved to the waiter to bring another round.

* * *

"Nick, could you hand me that box on the top shelf?" Some days Nora wished she were a bit taller. Nick and Nora were in the storage room in the rear of Spirit Song, unpacking new stock. Nick reached up and handed down the box. They heard the bells ring on the front door.

"I'll get it." Nick went up to the front to help the customer. Nora peeked out. It was a young woman with long hair dyed blue and purple. Nora liked to see someone expressing themselves in that way. Harmony could be quite conservative.

Nick greeted the woman and within a few minutes had her laughing and smiling as he showed her the jewelry in the display case.

It's great to have the extra help in the shop, Nora thought. Nick was proving himself invaluable to her. He was always on time, had great rapport with the customers, and was very organized. A quick learner, too. It had taken him only half an hour to master the till and cashout process.

Since the Grand Opening, she'd been dying to ask him questions about Jim Barnes. What kind of boss was he? What kind of person? So far she'd found Jim a bit hard to figure out.

Nora walked to the front of the shop, a box of candles in her arms. She began to arrange them on the shelves. She heard the front door open again. Nick would take care of it.

"Hello, stranger." The voice came from directly behind her.

Nora looked behind her and recognized her old schoolmate, Mike Gordon, a local real estate agent.

Oh brother! She forced a smile. Mike was dressed to impress, as usual. He looked like he had just stepped out of GQ magazine in his snowy white linen shirt, khaki pants and boat shoes.

"Hi, Mike. Nice to see you," she lied. He was harmless enough, but a bit of a blowhard and considered himself to be God's gift to women. Mike made a point of flirting with her every time he came in. She was friendly but deliberately aloof, which seemed to motivate Mike even more. The thrill of the chase, she supposed.

"You look extra fetching today, Nora. How about taking a break and coming out for coffee with me?"

"Thanks, Mike, but I have to put all this stock away, and I'm training Nick as well." She continued to place items on the shelf, hoping he'd take the hint.

"Oh right, the new guy." His tone was dismissive. Mike glanced over at the counter where Nick was serving the woman with the blue hair.

"Someday, Nora, you'll have to realize that all work and no play makes a dull girl."

Nora wanted to kick him but instead she shrugged her shoulders and reached down to pick up the empty box.

Mike winked at her. "Well, I'll leave you to it, then. Rain check?"

"Sure, sounds great." Nora figured that one of these days she would go out for coffee with Mike, just to get rid of him, but she didn't want to deal with him right now.

"I'll hold you to that, pretty lady!" Mike called over his shoulder as he went out.

Nora sighed. Nick came over as the other customer left the store.

"Who was that?" he asked.

"No one in particular, just an old friend from high school. If you could grab the new book stock and start putting it out, that would be great." Old friend was stretching it, but she had to say something.

"Will do." Nick went to the back room and returned with a box of books. He started stocking the shelf next to Nora.

They worked in silence for a while.

"Nick?"

"Umm…?"

"How do you like working at the garden center?" Nora hoped her inquiry sounded casual. She couldn't help being curious about Jim.

"I like it. It was pretty busy before the Grand Opening though. I mean crazy busy."

"Well, it worked out well. Jim had a really good turnout."

"For sure. He made a tidy profit, and I think he's already building a good client base in town. He's a good guy."

"Yes, Harmony has needed a garden center for a long time. Someone tried to start one about fifteen years ago, but it didn't take." She set out some tea candles and considered putting a few up at the till. Some customers might add it to their purchases as an afterthought.

They worked in silence for another few minutes.

Nora took the plunge. "I guess his wife must help him out as well."

Nick dusted off his hands.

"No wife," he replied. Nora dropped a candle, then quickly picked it up. She felt her face flush, but Nick didn't notice. "Only Jim and his little girl. She's a bit of a pest, but all right for a kid. She was a big help at the opening."

So he's not married. Nora didn't know what to do with that information. She would have to process it later.

"I like her," Nora said. "I think she's sweet. Well, that's the candles and books done. Still lots to shelve, but it really makes a difference having you here, Nick."

"Thanks. You have a lot of neat stuff in the shop. I've never worked in a place like this before."

"Well, you know if you have any questions about the stock or my services, you can ask anytime." She stood hands on hips, deciding what to shelve next.

"Thanks. I did want to ask about the…readings…is that what you call them?"

"That's right. I do tarot card readings for people. I'll give you a pamphlet that explains what those are."

Nick put the last book on the shelf. "Are you psychic? I hope you don't mind me asking."

Nora smiled. "Well, that's what some people call it. I guess I would say I am sensitive, and can see and hear some things that other people aren't able to. Sometimes I can provide guidance for people, through connecting to a higher source. The point is, there's nothing for people to be afraid of."

Nick looked thoughtful. "Maybe you could do a reading for me some time," he said.

"It would be my pleasure, Nick. One of the benefits of your job is a free reading from me every six months if you want it."

"Cool! Can we do one next week?" Nick looked hopeful.

"Sure, if you want. Here's the pamphlet I told you about. Look it over and then check in my appointment book on the desk to see when there's a spot available. Maybe give some thought ahead of time to what you would like to explore."

Nick had a wide grin on his face as he took the pamphlet from her hand. In her mind's eye, Nora suddenly saw the image of a young woman. She recognized Angelina from the hotel.

She smiled to herself. Of course. What else would pre-occupy a young man in his twenties?

CHAPTER SIX

Later that day, the bells on the door notified Nora that yet another customer had arrived. She looked up from her accounts book. Jim Barnes was walking in. Her heart rate stepped up a few beats.

"Hi, Nora." He looked tense as he approached the counter.

"Hi, Jim. What can I do for you?"

Jim looked down, stuck his hands in his pockets and looked at his shoes for a few seconds. "Glenna wants a reading," he said as he looked up again.

"Great!" Nora smiled at him but noticed he still looked uncomfortable. "When would she like to come in?"

Jim glanced around the shop and then made eye contact again. "We'll both be coming in, but the reading is for Glenna."

Nora got out her appointment book. "Even better. I have some openings this week or on the weekend if you like."

Jim took his hands out of his pockets. "Look, Nora. I don't really know how to say this, but I'm not too big on this new age stuff. I'm only coming because Glenna insists I come. Besides, I want to make sure she doesn't get...scared or anything. How does it work, anyway?" His eyebrows furrowed as he waited for her reply.

He's so edgy! Nora thought. *What happened to the friendly guy I talked to at the opening?*

"Nothing to be concerned about. I'll have Glenna shuffle some cards, pick out twelve and then I interpret the meaning of the cards for her. I try to always focus on the positive and the learning opportunities that the cards offer. I might see some people in her life, or some event that is coming up that she can prepare for. I might see some inner work she can do to be a better and happier person. It's really up to her what she takes away from it. I'm just a conduit for what you might call a Higher Power or Higher Spirit. It only takes about half an hour."

Jim looked dubious. Nora picked up a pamphlet from the counter and handed it to him.

"This is something I had printed to explain about tarot readings. Maybe you can look at it with Glenna."

"Yeah, maybe," Jim said, opening up the pamphlet.

Nora was getting slightly annoyed but trying not to show it. "It may become clearer once we start. And Glenna may have some things on her mind that she wants to ask about."

Jim stuffed the pamphlet in his coat pocket.

"Well, okay. We'll see. How about Saturday morning? I can pay you now if you want."

Nora smiled. "Don't worry about it. Maybe we'll call this an introductory session and you can pay for the next one?"

"No," Jim said bluntly. "You don't need to do that, Nora. I can pay."

Nora ignored him and Jim didn't push it.

"How about ten o'clock on Saturday?" she asked.

"Eleven would be better, if you can manage it," Jim answered. "Then I can take her out for lunch afterward."

"Eleven it is."

Nora wrote out an appointment card and handed it to him.

"I'll look forward to seeing the two of you."

Jim looked at the card, gave her a quick tight-lipped smile and made a beeline for the door.

Nora watched him exit the store. *Well, that was interesting.* He had been so gracious at the Grand Opening and now he was treating her like a stranger. She was attracted to him, but this encounter had left her feeling unsettled. She'd been dealing with non-believers her whole life, so why should Jim's skepticism bother her so much?

Well, she would see how things went on Saturday. She had no doubt about Glenna's enthusiasm, but she dreaded being under Jim's scrutiny as she opened herself to channel the cards. He had Glenna's best interests at heart, but she wished he'd chill out. *Who knows? He might even enjoy it.*

* * *

Jim Barnes took a sip of his coffee as Kevin MacNeal reached across the table to pick up the maple syrup, which he poured liberally over his pancakes. The two men often met up for breakfast at The Pancake House.

"Sweet enough for you, Kevin?" Jim chuckled. "It's more like you're having pancakes with your syrup!"

Kevin laughed. "I always loved lots of syrup, even as a kid," he confessed. "I would even dunk my toast in it. Maybe that's why I'm in love with a girl who owns a cupcake shop. I have a big sweet tooth, and Mandy is a phenomenal cook. Good thing I've always been active!"

Jim nodded his head at the waitress who was offering him more coffee. "Speaking of which, do you want to bike up one of the trails later? I've got Nick minding the store this afternoon and Glenna will be over at the Smythes' house."

"Sounds good," Kevin replied as he cut up his pancakes.

"We could…." Jim's attention was caught by a movement to his left. He turned in time to see Nora entering the restaurant with Mike Gordon.

They chose one of the booths near the window and ordered coffees. Immediately, Mike leaned across the table, focusing his entire attention on Nora and talking animatedly. Nora looked around the restaurant and spotted Jim and Kevin. Mike followed her gaze and began to wave at the two men.

"Hey, guys! How's it going?" Mike called loudly. He wanted everyone to see he was with Nora Fitzgerald.

Jim felt a flash of dismay. Mike Gordon? Really? He hadn't expected that Nora would go for that kind of man. Jim had only known Mike a short time, but it was clear that the guy had a very high opinion of himself. He was good-looking, but what on earth would a woman like Nora see in him besides that? Maybe she was more susceptible to a handsome face than he thought. He waved back cheerfully at Mike and Nora as if seeing them together didn't bother him one bit. Kevin waved a forkful of pancake.

Nora looks uncomfortable, Jim thought. She was glancing nervously toward his table. Maybe she didn't want anyone to witness her on a coffee date with Mike. He couldn't blame her, especially in a small town like Harmony. Even from this distance, Jim could hear Mike rattling on and on about his car, his clothes, his travel experiences. Nora was nodding politely, sharing the odd smile and responding occasionally to Mike's monologue.

"Jim? You were saying?" Kevin asked. Jim suddenly realized he'd stopped speaking mid-stream when he'd seen Mike and Nora together.

"Sorry, Kevin. So, we could meet at my place and then ride to the trail head?"

"I'll bring extra water," Kevin said. "Say in about an hour."

"Okay." Jim was looking over at Nora and Mike again. He drank up the rest of his coffee, said goodbye to Kevin and started for the front door.

"Jim!" Mike waved him over. "Have you met Nora Fitzgerald? She owns Spirit Song Books and Gifts on Main Street."

Jim and Nora stared at each other.

"Yes, we've met. How are you, Nora?" Jim's voice sounded cool even to his own ears.

"I'm fine, Jim. So, how's business?"

"Things are going great," Jim replied. There was an awkward silence.

Mike jumped in. "I've been trying to get Nora out for coffee. She works far too hard, so I made it my mission to get her out of the shop for a while." Mike made it sound like he and Nora were much closer than they actually were. Nora threw Mike a warning look.

"Well, good for you." Jim's tone was slightly sarcastic. Mike remained oblivious and kept talking about Nora's need to be looked after.

Jim cut in. "Sorry, but I'd better get going. I'm due to meet Kevin shortly for a bike ride."

"Excellent idea, Jim. If I wasn't so happily occupied…" Mike turned and winked at Nora, then turned back again. "…I'd go with you."

Nora looked up at Jim with an unreadable expression.

"Bye," Jim said curtly.

"Bye, Jim," Nora answered.

"See you later, buddy!" Mike gave a little salute then turned his full attention back to his date.

* * *

Sweaty and hot after the trail ride, Jim returned home to shower and change his clothes. He found himself thinking about the encounter in The Pancake House that morning. He still didn't get it. Mike Gordon was not someone he would ever imagine being a close friend of Nora's. From what he had seen so far, Nora was a pretty sensible type, and a little reserved. Mike was so…obnoxious. The whole thing made Jim uncomfortable. He decided to stop thinking about it.

Now, what did he need to take care of? He'd drop in at the hotel gardens to check the planters in the gazebo before collecting Glenna from the Smythes' and making her lunch.

Thirty minutes later, as he walked through the hotel gardens toward the gazebo, he saw an elderly man sitting on one of the benches near the fountain. The man looked at him, smiled and nodded. He couldn't remember having seen the man before. He nodded back in a friendly manner.

As he approached the gazebo, he was surprised to hear a woman singing softly. Whoever it was, it sounded good. She had a nice voice.

He arrived at the doorway of the gazebo and stood quietly for a moment, listening.

Nora looked up, startled.

"Jim!" She blushed and folded her hands in her lap. "I didn't see you. I was visiting Mrs. Arbuckle and I thought I'd take a few quiet moments in the gardens before heading back to the shop."

"Sorry," he said, a bit too gruffly. Why was his heart pumping so hard? "I didn't mean to disturb you. I'm checking the hanging baskets."

"Oh, they're beautiful!" Nora said, reaching up a hand to touch the trailing lobelia. "The gardens are so much nicer now that you're taking care of them."

"Thank you." His mind was racing, wondering what to say next.

"How was your trail bike ride?" Nora asked.

"Good. It's quite a workout. Kevin is pretty athletic. I had to hustle to keep up with him."

"Jim…" Nora hesitated.

"Yes?"

"I just wanted to say, seeing you this morning…well, Mike Gordon has been pestering me to go for a coffee for weeks."

"So he said." Jim started deadheading the flowers in the nearest basket so he wouldn't have to look at her.

"It's not like we're really dating, or anything. He's an acquaintance, that's all."

"None of my business." Did he sound too blunt?

He wanted to ask a lot more questions about Nora's relationship with Mike, but he repressed the urge to do so. He threw the debris from the basket over the side of the gazebo, dusted his hands off on his jeans and sat down beside her. They both looked out into the gardens. Suddenly he remembered something his father had said to him.

Son, a man and woman start their life together by looking directly at each other, but in time they end up standing side-by-side, looking outward together toward the future.

Well, here he was, sitting side-by-side with Nora Fitzgerald. And it felt good. He turned to look at her at the same time she glanced over at him.

Their eyes connected and a rush of pure emotion surged through him. He was breathless. He'd not felt such a thing since he'd first met Rachelle. Nora's shining eyes and warm smile held a promise that overwhelmed him. They gazed at each other for what seemed like a long time. He was conscious that a silent agreement was being made, an agreement of mutual interest and desire. Nora blushed and directed her gaze downward. He could see her hands shaking, then realized his own hands were trembling as well. *Oh God.*

"I've gotta go." Nora was standing and deliberately avoiding meet his eyes. "Goodbye, Jim." She dashed out of the gazebo and was already halfway across the lawn before he could respond.

Jim sat for a long time afterward, thinking things over.

Had Nora experienced the same reaction to him? Did she feel the same rush? He'd hadn't wanted to get involved with another woman until Glenna was older, yet here he sat considering that very possibility. His daughter deserved a woman in her life who would guide her into womanhood and teach her everything he could not. Although he managed to take care of their everyday needs, taking care of Glenna's emotional life was something a woman might be better equipped for. Did he want Nora in his life? More importantly, did he want her in both their lives?

CHAPTER SEVEN

On Saturday morning, Nora was waiting when Jim and Glenna entered Spirit Song Books and Gifts at exactly two minutes to eleven. She had arranged for Nick to cover the counter during the reading. Glenna ran up and gave her a big hug.

"We're not late are we?" Glenna smiled widely and looked toward the curtained-off room in the back of the shop.

"Right on time!" Nora smiled back at her at they released from the hug. Jim mumbled a greeting. *He doesn't look all that thrilled to be here*, Nora thought. She gestured toward the back room, walking in that direction.

After waving at Nick, Glenna grabbed Jim's hand and followed Nora to the back room. Nora held the purple velvet curtain aside for them to enter.

The room was dimly lit and held a round table surrounded by three chairs. The deep indigo tablecloth, patterned with stars, was topped with a small bowl of flowers and a tea light in a blue holder. An orange salt lamp glowed softly on a sideboard. Nora settled onto a chair and invited Jim and Glenna to take the chairs across from her. She carefully lit the tea light then reached for a small wooden box on the sideboard. Taking out a deck of tarot cards, she began to shuffle them. After a minute or two, she handed the cards to Glenna.

"There you go, honey. Shuffle the cards like I did, and while you are shuffling, think about what you would like to focus on in this reading."

Glenna eagerly took the cards and began shuffling them. She was a bit awkward and dropped a few cards, then picked them up again. She looked up. "I'm not too good at this," she said, glancing anxiously at her father.

Nora nodded encouragingly. "No worries, Glenna, you're doing fine! When you are ready, spread the cards out across the table face down and pick twelve cards."

Glenna spread out the cards and quickly picked out twelve. Nora took the rest of the cards, put them back in the box and put the box to one side. She picked up Glenna's cards and placed one card face up, a second card across it, a card above, a card below and a card on each side. She then placed a vertical row of cards, also face up on the right side of the cards in the middle.

"This is called the Celtic Cross," she said. "It's one of many ways to position the cards, but this pattern is my favorite."

Jim lifted his eyebrows. "I can't see what difference it would make."

"It's a tradition," Nora answered. "The placement of each card determines which part of your life the card speaks to."

"Do they tell you about love?" Glenna was looking at a card with a picture of a knight on it.

"Sometimes. They usually tell you what you need to know about or be aware of in the present. But yes, it can be love or school or friends or lots of other things."

Glenna looked over at her father. "Maybe you should get a reading too, Dad!"

Jim shook his head. "Not today, Sprout. This is your time."

"What comes up in the cards does not come from me," Nora explained. "I believe that your personal energy enters the cards when you shuffle them, and when you pick them. Your energy combines with a higher, or universal energy. Then I look at how each card relates to the other cards and I interpret the meaning. Take this card for instance." Nora pointed to the first card she had placed on the table. It showed a man, a woman and two children standing under a rainbow filled with golden cups.

"This card represents you, and where you are in your life right now. It's the Ten of Cups. A very positive card, indicating your recent arrival in a new place and a life filled with love, family and friendships."

"Wow! That's great!" Glenna exclaimed. Nora concentrated on the cards for another moment or two.

"I see you are making some adjustments right now, and that not all of those changes are easy for you. But I also see your strength of character and I know you can handle it."

"Anyone could say that," Jim commented, looking closely at Nora.

Nora looked back and smiled, but there was something in her eyes that let Jim know he should definitely butt out.

She continued. "I see trouble in the past. Someone you love has left and you feel sad about it."

"Maybe that's my mom," Glenna said. "She left and never came back, but I was pretty little so I don't remember it much." She glanced over at her father who was now frowning.

This startled Nora, but she hid it well. Her body tensed, but she forced herself to relax and put her attention back on the reading.

"It does seem to be a woman." Nora was silent for a few moments. "I see her in a tower, surrounded by a moat. She is not in connection with the world as we know it."

"That could be my grandma," Glenna said. "She passed away five years ago. She was seventy-five years old."

"I think this woman is younger," Nora said.

"Can we move on, please?" Jim's voice sounded defensive.

"Oh come on, Dad! This is fun!" Glenna gave her father a swat on the arm.

"If this person comes back into your life, you should be cautious." Nora frowned. "I don't feel she has your best interests in mind."

"Move on!" Suddenly, Jim's voice had a sharp edge. Nora wondered what he was so worked up about. She'd better take another tack.

"Here's some good news," she said to Glenna. "I see triumph ahead, maybe in a game or contest?"

"I have a soccer game this weekend. Maybe we'll win!" Glenna seemed excited.

Nora smiled. "Let me know when you're playing. I'll come watch."

"What's this card?" Glenna had her finger on a card showing a man standing on a cliff, carrying a bundle. A little dog stood by his side.

"That's the Fool. New beginnings," said Nora. "A very good card. It's all about new people in your life, new enterprises, letting go of the past."

Nora paused again.

"I do see some cards that indicate caution is necessary when it comes to travelling or being outdoors. It's always good to be prepared for whatever could happen, but don't let that hold you back from doing the things you want."

Jim sighed deeply and shifted in his chair.

"What's this card?" Glenna asked. She was pointing at a card with a majestic woman sitting on a throne.

"That's the Queen of Swords," Nora replied. "She is a symbol of a woman in power. A woman who sees things clearly and cuts through confusion. She gets straight to the point and speaks the truth. You can trust her."

"She sounds like you!" Glenna smiled.

"Are we done?" Jim was half-rising out of his chair.

CHAPTER EIGHT

"Henry! I'm home!" Nora dropped her purse on the foyer table along with her keys.

Nothing. Henry usually was waiting by the door when she got home.

"Henry?"

She ran up the stairs and called again. No Henry. Hurrying back down, she went to the kitchen. The back door was wide open and Henry was not in the yard. *This is crazy!* she thought. *I know I locked the back door this morning.*

Nora walked out into the yard and called Henry over and over. Nothing. She went to the side of the house and saw the gate was open. *Oh no, no, no!*

She rushed back to her car and began driving up and down the streets near her house, leaning out the window and calling Henry's name. Her stomach churned. *What if I can't find him?*

After cruising slowly through the neighborhood, she turned down Jasper Avenue. She spotted Jim outside the garden center, loading some plants in his truck. Nick was busy at the outdoor cash desk. Her pulse quickened as she recalled her last encounter with Jim. He'd been very distant. *Forget that, Nora, think about Henry!* She stopped the car and leaned out the window.

"Jim, have you or Nick seen Henry around here? He escaped from my yard."

Jim shoved the box he was holding into the back of his truck and shut the gate. "No, I haven't seen him. Nick, have you seen a black dog around?"

Nick shook his head. Jim walked up to Nora's car window.

Nora bit her lip. "I've searched my neighborhood, but I'm scared he might have gone downtown or to the park. He's very active and can run really fast. He doesn't know much about traffic."

"I'll come with you if you want," Jim said, looking concerned. "I can help you search."

She didn't question why he wanted to come with her. All she knew was that she needed him with her. "Thanks, Jim. I could use the help. Hop in."

Jim yelled to Nick that he would be gone for a while, then walked around to the passenger side and got in. As she drove on, Nora was keenly aware of Jim's presence beside her. Her mind again went back to their meeting in the gazebo. He hadn't seemed so distant then. *Stop it. Henry is what you need to think about right now.*

They searched downtown, near the school and at Harmony Park, then headed down Cougar Road until they reached Harmony Creek. Nora stopped the car. They both got out and began walking toward the hotel gardens.

Jim cupped his hands around his mouth. "Henry!"

"Henry, where are you?" Nora's eyes began to fill. Her throat tightened. Henry was her dearest friend now that her parents and sister had left town. She couldn't bear the thought that he was in danger or had already been harmed. Tears started to trickle down her cheeks. Immediately she felt Jim's arm wrap around her shoulders.

"Don't worry, we'll find him, Nora." Jim's voice was gentle. She remembered the look they had exchanged in the gazebo. She knew she could trust him.

"Thank you, Jim." She looked up into his face, and before either could grasp what was happening he bent forward and kissed her. It was a sweet, consoling kiss. Nora pulled away and looked up into his eyes.

"Nora, I'm so sorry. I don't know why I did that." Jim looked guilty and repentant.

Nora blushed. "It's okay. I kind of liked it."

"Me, too." Jim replied, looking deeply into her eyes. "But we need to look for Henry."

"Yes...yes. Of course."

They continued to gaze at each other for a few moments, before being startled out of their reverie by the sound of a dog barking.

"Henry?" Nora turned and saw Henry racing toward them, his curly tail wagging.

"Henry!" The dog leaped up on Nora, then raced around the two of them, barking happily. "Thank God!" Nora squatted down, wrapped her arms around Henry and held him close.

"Henry, buddy, where have you been?" Jim gave the shaggy head a pet.

Nora looked up and in the distance she could see Mr. Arbuckle in the gazebo, waving at her. He was smiling. Jim picked up a stick and threw it for Henry to fetch.

Mr. Arbuckle - you old fox! Nora thought. *I bet you had something to do with all this!*

Nora and Jim loaded Henry into the back seat of the car and Nora drove back to the garden center. Jim stepped out and walked around to the driver's window.

"I enjoyed our…time together. To be continued?" He looked meaningfully at Nora.

A thrill rippled down her spine. "To be continued. Thanks again for your help, Jim. I don't know what I would have done if I'd lost Henry."

"I'll give you a call." Jim smiled back. He reached up and gently brushed a strand of hair away from her face, then turned and walked back to his truck.

Nora watched him go. *Things were getting interesting.*

"All right, you rascal," she said to Henry. "Home we go!"

"Woof!" said Henry.

* * *

The next day, as Jim was potting plants in the greenhouse, his emotions were in turmoil. Working helped. Putting his hands in the rich damp crumble of peaty soil always grounded him. He did his best thinking while gardening, and he had a lot to think about today.

Kissing Nora yesterday had aroused unexpected desires. The urge to touch her had been irresistible. It seemed so absolutely right and natural at the time to comfort her in her distress. He certainly hadn't planned to kiss her as well. But her tears had touched him deeply, and all his suppressed longing for her had taken over. As he held her slender form in his arms, his body ached for more. The light floral scent of her hair and the silkiness of her lips elevated his senses. He'd barely been able to subdue the impulse to take it to the next level.

He knew now that he'd been in denial about his feelings for Nora. From the first day they met, he'd been deeply attracted to her but had deliberately pushed away his yearning to explore that attraction. At times, he'd been downright rude to her. He'd denied his own needs to focus on the two things he did best: parenting Glenna and building his new business. The knowledge that he'd taken the next step in getting closer to Nora filled him with a mixture of joy and apprehension.

He'd come to Harmony hoping to build a new life for himself and Glenna. Above all, he wanted simplicity and freedom from the emotionally charged months before and during his divorce. Rachelle had found a good divorce lawyer and been surprisingly successful in throwing obstacles in his way. Winning custody of Glenna had not been a problem due to Rachelle's criminal history, but his ex-wife had continued to put claims on their mutual property, which is why he'd sold first his house in Olds, and then his very successful horticultural business. He'd been forced to divide most of the profits with Rachelle.

He was still feeling burned from the divorce, even though it had been eight years ago. After the papers were finalized, he and four-year-old Glenna had moved to Calgary. He'd found a good day care and kindergarten for her and later an elementary school. He'd worked hard during those years in Calgary, adding to the money he had banked from the sale of his property in Olds. There was no time for anything else. Certainly no time for a social life. Eventually, he had enough saved to allow him to move and start a new business in Harmony.

Harmony had been the obvious choice for relocating. While in Calgary, he and Glenna often visited the mountains, and he'd taken a special liking to Harmony, the town where they usually stopped for ice cream on the way home. Harmony had all the amenities he was looking for, including a good school for Glenna and excellent prospects for starting a business. Before his arrival, Harmony residents had a one-hour drive to the nearest greenhouse. The townspeople had welcomed him with open arms, and after the success of the Grand Opening, he knew he'd made the right decision.

His thoughts returned to Nora. He hadn't expected to find love in his new life. Was he ready to commit to that? After Rachelle, he'd been convinced that he would never want to be with a woman again. God knows he'd been through enough, and he wasn't the type for one-nighters or casual relationships.

But Nora Fitzgerald was unlike anyone he'd met before. For one thing, she was everything Rachelle was not. Beautiful, kind, responsible, independent and a successful business owner. What's more, Glenna adored her and talked about her constantly.

Jim knew what he had to do. He had to explore this new relationship. He dusted the soil off his hands and swept the debris off the potting bench. He stopped briefly at the sink to wash his hands and headed for his office.

It took only a few seconds to dial the number.

"Hello, Nora, it's Jim. I'm phoning to see if you might like to join me for dinner on Friday."

Nora's unhesitating acceptance confirmed his decision. He hung up the phone and sat in his office, looking out the window at the rows and rows of plants he had carefully propagated. If he knew one thing, it was that life and beauty could come from planting a single seed.

CHAPTER NINE

Nora scanned her closet for several minutes before pulling out a sleeveless blue silk dress with a V-shaped neckline. She laid the dress across her bed, next to the lacy Victoria's Secret underwear she wore only for special occasions. Back at the closet, she reached down and grabbed a pair of silver slingback sandals which she placed on the floor beside the bed.

Henry, curled up on the carpet, watched with interest, thumping his tail whenever she came near.

Her hair was still damp from her bubble bath and hung in tendrils down her back. After bathing, she had dabbed a little perfume on her earlobes, neck and wrists and carefully applied her makeup. Nora opened the jewelry box on her dresser and chose a pair of dangling silver earrings with a moon and star design set with tiny crystals. She placed them on her dresser and pulled out a simple silver locket which she fastened around her neck. Nice. Not too glitzy. Simple and chic.

She blow-dried her hair and then dressed slowly. Finally, she put on the earrings. Another check in the mirror. She was pleased with what she saw.

Normally she was fairly calm before a date, but this time she felt different. Butterflies? Yes, definitely. Lots of butterflies.

Jim sounded so calm when he'd phoned to ask her out. She had been surprised by the call, and had found herself trembling with excitement as she hung up the receiver. Not long ago, she'd had a difficult time determining whether he liked her or not. His behavior toward her had varied to the point that she was unsure what to expect from him. But the memory of their kiss in the park filled her with anticipation. As unexpected as his embrace had been, her body had instantly responded. Even her worry about Henry had left her for several seconds as she took in the warmth of his lips, his masculine scent and the strength of his body. It had seemed so natural to nestle in his arms and savor the warmth of his protective embrace.

She glanced at the clock. He'd arranged to pick her up at seven p.m. The dinner reservations were for seven-fifteen. She had to credit him for his choice of restaurant. The Foothills Dining Room at the Thurston Hotel was very elegant and had the best food in town.

The doorbell rang and Henry ran barking to the front of the house. Nora slipped on her sandals and made her way to the door. Jim Barnes stood holding a bouquet of pink roses in his hand.

He was dressed in a well-fitting dark gray suit, a pale blue shirt and navy tie. He looked polished and very sexy. The clothes brought out the intense blue of his eyes. Nora was a bit surprised by his appearance. Previous to this she had only seen him in jeans and work shirts. Looking at him now, she reflected that he could be a CEO in a big city company.

She greeted him with a smile. "Hi, Jim, would you like to come in for a minute?"

"Hi, Nora. Thanks, I will. Hey, boy!" Jim ruffled the hair on Henry's head. Henry was already nuzzling Jim's hand. That was a good sign. Henry was very particular about visitors.

Nora took the bouquet from Jim's hands. "These are gorgeous. How thoughtful. I'll put them in some water."

"You look lovely, Nora."

"Thank you, kind sir." Nora beamed at him. "You look very nice yourself. I'll be right back. Make yourself at home."

Jim carefully cleaned his shoes on the mat before stepping into the living room and settling into a chair. In a few minutes, Nora came back with a crystal vase filled with the roses. She placed them on the mantel.

"There we go, pride of place!" she said. "Shall we go?"

Jim stood up and moved quickly to the door to hold it open for her. Nora turned and commanded Henry to sit and stay. "Be a good dog, Henry," she said. Henry gave a sigh of resignation.

"I'm sorry, all I've got is my truck," Jim explained sheepishly.

"Your truck is just fine," Nora reassured him.

Jim opened the passenger door and offered her a hand so she could step up more easily. She settled into her seat as he gently closed the passenger door and went around to the driver's side.

"All good?" he asked.

"All good." Nora could smell his cologne as he got into the cab, subtle and masculine and in no way overwhelming. She appreciated that.

Within minutes they were at the hotel and Jim jumped out to run around and open her door. "I'll park the truck and be right with you," he said, offering his hand to help her step down.

Nora nodded, stepped down and walked into the lobby. All she could think about was how great Jim looked. Her face lit up when Jim came in and offered her his arm. A true gentleman.

A few moments later the waiter was showing them to their table in the Foothills Dining Room. Jim pulled out Nora's chair then seated himself across from her. The table was elegantly laid with fine silver, china and linen. A small silver bowl of white roses was flanked by candles in crystal holders on each side. The waiter brought the menus.

"Everything looks good!" Jim commented, glancing through the menu. "This is the first time I've been here."

"I recommend the Alberta Angus beef," Nora said. "And be sure to leave room for dessert, you'll be glad you did!"

"I'll do that." After some consultation, Jim ordered a bottle of merlot. The waiter brought it and Jim tested it.

He nodded. The waiter poured generously. They clinked glasses and took the first sip.

"Very nice," Nora remarked. She glanced up to see Jim looking at her. *He's so attractive*, Nora thought.

"I don't know if you noticed, Nora, but you made quite a sensation in the lobby!"

Nora blushed. "I didn't." She took another sip of her wine. "I'm enjoying myself, Jim."

"Me, too," Jim said, looking around. "It's a nice dining room. This is really the first time I've had a chance to see more of the hotel."

Nora tried to remember the last time she had been on a civilized and elegant date like this. She couldn't. "It's good to be here with you. But I have to say, Jim, I wasn't sure what to expect."

Jim looked at her quizzically.

Nora continued. "The few times we've met, you seemed to be in a different mood each time, and I wasn't sure why."

Jim frowned. "I'm sorry. It definitely had nothing to do with you. I have no excuse, really, other than being unsure of myself."

"Of course," Nora said. "I suppose I'd like to understand where you are coming from."

Jim ran his finger along the edge of the table and looked thoughtful.

"I guess I should tell you I'm divorced. It was eight years ago when Glenna was a toddler. It wasn't an amicable divorce, in fact it was a nightmare, but Glenna and I have made a new start in Harmony."

"I'm sorry you had to go through that, Jim." Nora was sympathetic. Obviously he'd been through a lot. "You're lucky to have Glenna. She's a sweet girl. You've done a good job with that one."

Jim's face lit up. "Thank you. I'm very proud of her."

"You should be," Nora replied. "I always enjoy her visits to the store."

"As long as she isn't bothering you," he said anxiously.

"Not at all. I'll tell her if I'm too busy."

Jim poured a bit more wine in both their glasses. They sipped in silence for a few moments.

"This is the first date I've had since the divorce," Jim confessed.

"It's been a long time for me, as well." Nora put her glass down and gently placed her hand over Jim's on the table.

Jim laced his fingers into hers. "You're a very special woman, Nora Fitzgerald," he said. "The truth is, I've liked you from the beginning, but I wasn't sure what was happening with you. Especially when I saw you with Mike Gordon."

Nora laughed. "Mike Gordon! I went out for coffee with him to get him to stop bothering me!"

"Good," said Jim, pressing her hand. "I have a chance then?"

Nora looked at him and pressed back. "You do."

The waiter arrived with their food. Angus steak, baked potato and corn for Jim, chicken and Caesar salad for Nora.

"Yum!" Nora said.

"To us," Jim said, and they clinked glasses again.

* * *

Nora felt ecstatic as they stepped out into the hotel gardens. It was the perfect finish to the evening. Soft fairy lights shone throughout the grounds, strategically placed to give the gardens a subtle glow. The night air, filled with the fragrance of flowers, was mysterious and intoxicating. They stood for a few moments watching the sweep of the night sky against the outline of the mountains, then made their way to the gazebo to enjoy the view. They sat together looking out, as they had on the day when Jim had found her there singing to herself.

"What a wonderful job you've done on the gardens, Jim," Nora commented. "The flowers are amazing, and it's like a fairyland with all the lights." She turned toward him. "Now, tell me more about yourself."

"Not too much to tell," Jim explained. "Working with plants has always been part of my life. When I was a kid I had my own little garden at home. During high school, I ran a part-time business taking care of people's yards. So going to the horticultural college in Olds was a no-brainer for me. Later I started my first garden center, got married and had Glenna. After that, well, things got complicated with Rachelle, my ex-wife. We decided to split up. I moved to Calgary with Glenna after the divorce and worked in a horticultural company there. Glenna and I used to come up to the mountains on weekends, and we liked it, so I made a five-year plan to move here and start a business."

"Judging from the Grand Opening, you won't have any lack of work!" Nora said with a grin.

"Yes, I think you're right." Jim reached over and took Nora's hand. Their eyes met. "Now tell me your story, Nora."

"I grew up in Harmony," Nora responded. "My father was a biology teacher at the high school," she explained. "My mother worked part-time as a clerk in various shops in town. We had a good life. Dad retired early because of a health condition and my parents moved to Palm Springs a few years ago. I have a sister, Colleen, who is married and lives in Vancouver. We all keep in touch with Skype and Facebook. Are your parents still in Olds?"

Jim stroked her palm with his fingers. "Yes. Dad is a pharmacist. He relaxes after work by spending time in the garden. He started me growing things when I was about four. Our yard overflowed with flowers. We grew all our own vegetables, and my mom canned everything for winter. I was the only kid, but my parents never spoiled me. I had to work for everything I got. My parents made sure of that."

They were silent for a few minutes. Jim still had hold of Nora's hand. Ever so gently, he reached up and brushed a lock of her hair behind her ear.

"You're so beautiful, Nora." His voice was soft, his eyes glistening with desire.

Nora was suddenly having trouble breathing. "Thank…you…" she murmured, her heart beating madly. Her hands began to shake. Jim moved closer on the gazebo bench.

"Nora?" He reached up again and turned her face toward him. "I'd…like to kiss you. Is that okay?"

Nora looked at him, smiled shyly and nodded.

He drew her toward him and engaged her in a long, passionate kiss. Her body surrendered completely to his embrace. It was…delicious. She was immediately aroused and wanted more, much more. One of Jim's arms slipped around her waist and pulled her even closer. His hand went to the back of her head, caressing her hair and pressing her more deeply into the kiss. She closed her eyes and took in the smell of his skin. A mixture of delectable man-scent with a clean whiff of soap and cologne. Her hands went around his neck as the kiss grew more and more intense.

Finally, they pulled back from each other. Both were breathing heavily. They gazed into each other's eyes, sharing a smile of secret delight. Jim once again drew her closer as he leaned back against the bench. Nora relaxed her body against his, dropping her head onto his shoulder as he cradled her in his arms.

For a long time, they rested there in silence, looking out at the starlight and the mountains beyond.

CHAPTER TEN

Rachelle Barnes stepped off the bus, dropped her bag on the ground and immediately put a cigarette to her lips, curving her hand around the lighter to keep out the wind.

She took a few puffs and looked around at the mountains, unimpressed. *If you've seen one big hunk of rock, you've seen them all. Who would want to live in this godforsaken place? Jim must be out of his mind.* She preferred the hustle of the city and all it had to offer. Finally getting parole made her determined to land in a place with a ready supply of booze, coke and sexy men. It had been a long eight years. This place looked pretty tame but if she played her cards right, she would soon be heading for Vancouver and the bright lights with a wad of cash in her pocket.

One of the reasons her parole hearing had gone so well was because of extra favors she had done for the guards - providing sex in exchange for them testifying on her behalf. Of course they went for it. *Those idiots.*

Now she had to get a foothold in Jim's new life. Harmony - what a stupid name. Sounded like something from a freakin' fairy tale. Jim would pick a place like this - he was such a nerd. She wondered what Glenna looked like now. She must be what, ten? That kid would make it way easier for her to get whatever she could from Jim. Quite a bargaining chip. She smiled to herself and blew a couple of smoke rings.

Okay. Where should she go first? Maybe a drink, then find out where Jim's business was. She headed for the pub she could see across the street from the bus depot.

At The Wobbly Dog, she found a table facing the door and ordered a neat whiskey with a beer chaser. She asked the waitress if she had a smartphone she could borrow to look up an address and the waitress obligingly fished her phone out of her apron pocket. Rachelle surfed through the Harmony town webpages. There it was. Jim's Yard and Garden Center. Elk Street and Jasper Avenue. That had to be him.

After handing the phone back, Rachelle leaned back and lit another cigarette. A couple of men were sitting at the bar. They kept turning around to look at her. She smiled at them and leaned over to adjust her shoe so they could get a full view of her ample cleavage. Pretty soon one of them came over and offered to buy her a drink. She accepted. The man sat close to her as his friend looked on with amusement. After a few minutes of conversation, Rachelle offered to show him a good time for fifty dollars. He acted kind of surprised but agreed to meet her in his car out back. Easy money. *What a hick. I guess they don't get many women like me in Harmony.*

* * *

When Jim drove into the parking lot at the garden center that afternoon he saw a petite blonde woman talking to Nick at the cash desk. It took him only a few seconds to recognize her.

Oh God. Rachelle! His heart plummeted. *No!* The thing he had been dreading had come true. What was she doing here? What did she want? His mind raced. Glenna! He must protect Glenna at all costs.

He jumped out of his truck and walked quickly to the cash desk.

"Jim! Baby!" Rachelle flung herself at him and threw her arms around his neck. Jim recoiled and took a step back. Nick stared. "Oh Baby, it's so good to see you again!"

Jim took Rachelle's wrists and pushed her hands away. "Stop it."

"Jimmy, aren't you glad to see me? It's been so long!"

"What are you doing here, Rachelle?" Jim made sure his tone was cold and unwelcoming.

"Well, where else would I go except to my family!" Rachelle tilted her head and smiled coyly.

"We're not family, Rachelle. We're divorced." Jim stepped behind the counter so it was between the two of them.

"That doesn't mean we don't have history, Jimmy."

Jim shook his head. "It means you are no longer my wife, Rachelle, and I don't want you coming around here and causing trouble. The papers were final."

Rachelle put her hands on the counter and leaned toward him. "C'mon Jimmy! Have a heart! I have nowhere else to go."

Jim saw the quizzical look on Nick's face. Coming out from behind the counter and taking Rachelle by the elbow, Jim steered her out of the store and into the street. "Just go, Rachelle. There's nothing for you here."

Rachelle pouted and put her hands on her hips. "What about my baby girl?" she asked sweetly.

"Don't you dare go near Glenna!" Jim thundered. "You stay away from her; you hear? She doesn't need your crap in her life! I have custody, and you know it! Stay away!"

Rachel scowled. "Maybe we should leave that up to her, Jimmy. She's probably old enough to make up her own mind."

Jim looked at her with disgust. "You couldn't care less about her."

"We'll see. We'll see." Rachelle walked a few steps away, picked her bag back up off the ground and turned back to face him. "I suppose staying at your house is out of the question?" she inquired.

"You're damn right it is." Jim couldn't believe this was happening. *How did she find him?*

"Well, no problem." Rachelle was still smiling. "I'll find my own little digs here in this crappy little backwater of a town."

"Hit the road Rachelle - or else!" Jim barked.

"Or else what? You can't tell me what to do, Jimmy - remember, you're not my husband anymore." Rachelle turned and started walking away, deliberately swaying her hips in a provocative way. She stopped and looked back, flashing him the finger. "See you around, Jimmy boy!"

"You stay away from Glenna!" Jim yelled after her. Rachelle ignored him and kept walking. He watched her as she sashayed down Elk street, turned left onto Jasper Avenue and headed toward Main Street.

Oh God! What was he going to do? He had to talk to Glenna before Rachelle did. And what if Nora heard about this? Just as things were going so well for them. Jim sat down on the bench in front of the store, leaned forward and held his head in his hands.

* * *

"Henry! Time for a walk, buddy!" Nora called out.

Henry came dashing up to the front hall where Nora waited for him, leash and collar in hand. He danced around her with excitement and then stood patiently as she fastened his collar around his neck. Nora stuffed some plastic bags in one pocket and a small bag of dog cookies in the other. She opened the door and Henry lunged out, dragging her behind him.

Nora laughed. "Easy there, Henry! I'd like to get to the park without falling on my face!"

She headed down Caribou Street and turned left onto Sunshine Avenue. They passed the Community

Center. Once they were on the edge of town behind the Thurston Hotel in the dog park, she released Henry, who raced around for a few minutes then trotted happily in front of her, sniffing as he went. She saw a white-haired man sitting on one of the benches ahead. He turned his head, looked at her, then waved. Mr. Arbuckle.

Henry raced up to the bench and tried to lick Mr. Arbuckle's hand, but ended up licking the air.

"Henry, when will you learn that Mr. Arbuckle is different?"

She could see Walter Arbuckle silently laughing at Henry's efforts to be friendly.

Nora sat down on the bench, took a breath and opened her psychic channels to receive whatever it was the late Mr. Arbuckle wanted to share. These paranormal encounters only happened when he had something important to convey.

His words came into her mind.

How are you, Nora?

I'm fine, and you? she answered silently.

Fine, dear. Things are looking up for you.

Nora blushed. She knew Mr. A was referring to her evening with Jim.

He's a good man, Nora. Don't let this one go.

I won't, she replied.

Dear, I've something to tell you.

Yes?

Trouble is here. Trouble for you and Jim. Be ready. Be careful.

What is it? Nora was immediately concerned.

Be strong. Trust him, Nora. Trust him. He always tells the truth.

Nora twisted the dog leash in her hands. Why wouldn't she trust him? She looked around and Mr. A was gone. Henry barked.

Nora got up and continued on, wondering what kind of trouble she and Jim were heading into.

CHAPTER ELEVEN

At four in the afternoon, Rachelle Barnes made her way to the Elementary School and sat on a bench beside the soccer field. She lit a cigarette, watched the kids running around the field and went over her plan in her mind.

It hadn't taken much to figure out where she might locate her daughter in Harmony. She knew Jim had always been a big soccer fan and logic told her that he would have gotten Glenna involved in the sport. She'd used the computer in the town library to find Glenna's Facebook profile. *Hmmm. Not a half-bad looking kid. Takes after her mother.* Then she'd looked up the Harmony junior soccer league schedule for July.

The soccer practice ended and Rachelle stubbed out her cigarette.

She spotted Glenna right away, chatting happily with a group of girls. Rachelle approached them. "Hi there," she said.

The girls smiled back. She saw them looking at her with cautious curiosity. She was a stranger in town. Rachelle turned her attention to Glenna. "Glenna Barnes?" she asked.

"Yes…?" Glenna looked surprised.

"Can I have a word with you?"

Glenna was hesitant. "I guess…right here?"

"How about at that bench over there?" Rachelle pointed. Glenna followed her to the bench and they sat down.

"What's all this about?" Glenna asked, twisting her hands together nervously.

"Well, this may come as a little bit of a shock," Rachelle reached over and took one of Glenna's hands. "I'm your momma, Baby."

Glenna jerked her hand away and stared at the strange woman. "What?!" Glenna's brow was furrowed.

"I'm your momma."

Glenna continued to stare.

"My mom left me and my dad a long time ago," Glenna said.

"I came back, Baby. Aren't you glad to see me?" Rachelle asked.

"I don't...know." Glenna looked down again. "I don't know you."

Rachelle pulled a picture out of her purse. It showed a younger Jim Barnes holding his baby daughter. She handed it to Glenna. "See? This is you when you were just a little bit of a thing."

Glenna stared at the picture for several minutes in confusion. She handed it back to Rachelle. "I've gotta go home now." She stood up. "I need to talk to my dad."

"Okay, Baby Girl. We can catch up later. I'm staying at a motel down the highway a bit. You go talk to your dad and I'll see you soon."

* * *

Glenna walked toward home, ignoring her friends waving goodbye. She caught her breath when a car screeched to a halt on her left. She'd stepped off the curb without looking.

"Hey, kid! Be careful and pay attention!" She felt her face redden as the driver called out a warning.

"Hi, Glenna!" the next-door neighbor called. Without acknowledging her, Glenna made her way onto the front porch and used her key to open the front door. She dropped her soccer kit bag on the floor.

Dad isn't home yet. Without taking her coat off, she went up to her bedroom and lay down on the bed, staring at the ceiling.

* * *

"Glenna?" Jim called when he arrived home. He saw the soccer bag lying on the floor near the front door. Glenna's coat wasn't on the hook. She must be out with Dolly Smythe.

Jim went into the kitchen and opened a beer from the fridge. He took a few swigs, put it down on the table and went upstairs to change his clothes. As he was passing Glenna's bedroom, he heard a soft sound. He looked in.

Glenna was lying on her bed, tears streaming down her cheeks. "Daddy?" she said in a weak voice.

Immediately alarmed, Jim strode in and put his hand on his daughter's head. "Honey, what's wrong? Are you sick?"

"Daddy…" Glenna sobbed in earnest. Jim cradled her head against his chest and let her cry. Then he held her at arm's length and looked into her face. "Glenna, honey, what is it?"

"I met…a lady…who said…she was my…momma." Glenna stammered between sobs.

"What? Where was this, Glenna?"

"At the school…she was at the school!" Glenna was hysterical.

Jim held her closer. "Okay, okay, everything's gonna be all right, Sprout."

"Is it really her? She showed me a picture of you." Glenna looked up at Jim with a tear-streaked face and pleading eyes.

"Yes, Glenna." Jim answered gently. "She came to see me yesterday, and I was trying to find a way to tell you. I'm sorry you found out this way. I know it's very confusing."

"What is she doing here?" Glenna demanded, her voice cracking.

"I think she wants to see you, Glenna. She is your mother, after all. I know she left us a long time ago, but she's here now. We need to figure it out together."

"I didn't even…recognize…her," Glenna sobbed.

"That's natural. You haven't see her in a long, long time. Since you were a little girl."

Jim continued to hold her in his arms for a while. Gradually Glenna's breathing slowed and she quieted down.

"Let's go down to the kitchen and have a snack," he suggested. "It will do us good."

Glenna nodded and wiped her face with her hands.

They made their way downstairs to the kitchen where Jim poured Glenna a tall glass of milk and placed some cookies on a plate in front of her. He picked up his beer and slowly sipped it, watching his daughter.

Glenna drank her milk but ignored the cookies. She stared at the table.

Finally, she looked up at Jim. "What are we going to do?" she asked.

"We're going to deal with this one day at a time," he answered. "I'll talk to your mother and work something out. You don't have to see her if you don't want to, Glenna. All you have to do is say so."

"I don't know." Glenna shook her head.

"Don't worry about it right now. Dad will take care of it. Let's put on a movie and I'll order pizza. We'll have a quiet night in, okay?"

"Okay." Glenna sounded tired and depressed.

As they finished the pizza, Jim put on Glenna's favorite movie. Glenna had barely eaten. As the movie began, she rested her head on her father's shoulder. Soon she fell fast asleep, exhausted by her ordeal.

Jim was furious at Rachelle, and furious at himself.

Why hadn't he told Glenna right away that Rachelle was in town? Why did she have to find out this way? Now he would have to figure out how best to handle the situation and protect Glenna. He hoped there wouldn't be any long-term psychological damage.

Looking down, he gazed tenderly upon his sleeping daughter's face. So innocent. She didn't deserve this. He kissed the top of her head.

CHAPTER TWELVE

Nora knew it was Jim on the phone. Since their romantic dinner at the hotel, Jim had called almost every day to chat. Every call left Nora feeling elated but she was still a bit nervous when the phone rang. As a rule, she knew ahead of time exactly who was calling. That was just part of her psychic ability. But she was always glad and excited when it was Jim.

"Hello, Nora."

"Jim! How are you?"

There was a silence on the other end of the line.

Oh oh, Nora thought, *what's up? What if Jim has decided he isn't really interested?* Until this moment she hadn't realized how important it was to her.

"Nora…I have to talk to you about something," Jim began hesitantly.

Nora's heart dropped. Maybe there was someone else?

"Yes?"

"I wasn't expecting this, but my ex-wife has arrived in town. I asked her to stay away, but she's insisting on seeing Glenna."

Nora felt confused. Was there any possibility that Jim would want to reconcile with his ex? Her voice was shaky as she answered him.

"Oh…I see. I'm not sure what to say, Jim."

"You don't need to say anything," Jim quickly replied. "We're divorced but Rachelle has a way of causing trouble. I wanted to warn you about it."

"Um...okay." Nora thought quickly. "Look Jim, maybe it's better if we don't see each other for a while, at least until you sort things out with her."

There was a long silence on the other end of the line. "Jim?"

"Okay, sure, Nora. Whatever you think is best. Well, I better head to work. I'll talk to you later." And with that Nora heard the phone click and go dead.

Now you've done it, Nora Fitzgerald. Why had she suggested a break? *Stupid. Stupid. Stupid! Now Jim will think I'm brushing him off because of his past, and that's the last thing I want him to think.*

She wondered how she would react if she ran into Rachelle. She knew Rachelle had left when Glenna was only four. How would it affect Glenna meeting her mother after all this time? She would hate to see Glenna or Jim get hurt. Should she phone Jim back? No, better not. She needed to give him space and stay out of it. Suddenly she felt cold all over.

"Henry!" Nora held Henry close and took comfort in his presence.

* * *

Jim immediately regretted hanging up the phone so abruptly. What would Nora think of him? He'd been so

93

disappointed when she suggested taking a break. He didn't know how things would turn out with Rachelle. Most of all, he didn't want Nora getting involved or meeting his ex. He knew Rachelle would try and poison anything good he had found in Harmony. That was just her style.

The phone rang. Jim jumped at the sound and grabbed the receiver.

"Hello, Nora?" he blurted.

"Jimmy? Who's Nora?"

Jim slammed his hand on the wall. "Damn it, Rachelle, why did you go see Glenna before talking to me? Where are you?" He began to pace the kitchen floor.

"Down the road a bit, at a motel. She's a sweet girl, Jimmy."

He sat down in a chair at the kitchen table. "She's a very confused and unhappy girl at the moment, thanks to you."

"Oh, she'll get over it." Rachelle sounded indifferent. "I want to take her out for dinner and get to know her better."

"You're not taking her anywhere without me coming along." Jim was gripping the phone so hard his knuckles were white. If Rachelle kept trying to force herself into their lives he couldn't answer for the consequences.

"Geez, Jimmy, chill out! She has a right to see her mama, after all." Rachelle wheedled.

"But you have no right to see her unless I say so."

"Really, Jimmy? What about when she comes of age in a couple of years? Maybe she'll want to try living with me." It was a threat, pure and simple.

Jim seethed. He tightened his grip on the phone even more. "Don't make any long-term plans, Rachelle," he cautioned.

"Come on, Jimmy. One dinner. What could it hurt?" Rachelle was all sweetness. Oh, he was very familiar with that tone.

A lot, Jim thought. But he knew that putting up roadblocks might make both Rachelle and Glenna more determined to see each other.

"I'll talk to Glenna and see what she says," he offered. "But remember who has custody and behave yourself."

"Perfect, Jimmy! How about Friday night?" He could hear the triumph in her voice.

"As I said, I'll be talking to Glenna first. What is your cell number?"

Jim jotted down the number as Rachelle continued. "You'll see, Jimmy! We'll be like one happy family again."

God forbid. "Don't even go there, Rachelle. This is a one-time thing."

Rachelle laughed. "Of course it is, honey, of course. I'll look forward to your call."

"Goodbye, Rachelle."

"Goodbye, Jimmy. Can't wait!"

Rachelle hung up and Jim stared at the phone in his hand. What had he gotten himself and Glenna into?

* * *

Big Joe had been the bouncer at The Wobbly Dog for more years than he cared to remember, and he'd seen a lot, but that little blonde who had come in earlier took the cake.

Dressed like a ten-dollar hooker, the woman took a seat at the bar, ordered a beer and glanced around. The pub was very full for a Thursday night. She turned her attention back to the bartender, who was bustling around filling orders. *I better keep an eye on that one,* Big Joe reflected. *I know trouble when it walks in the door.*

"What does it take to have a good time in this town?" the woman asked the bartender provocatively.

"Well, if you're outdoorsy, there's lots to do," the bartender explained. "Hiking, camping, canoeing and kayaking in the summer, snowshoeing, skiing and boarding in the winter." He stood drying glasses in front of her.

"Not that kind of fun!" She rolled her eyes at him. "Any gambling joints?"

"Not really. We have some VLTs. People come here mostly for the outdoor activities."

"Booorrring!" The woman tossed back the last of her beer and tapped her glass on the counter. The bartender quickly replaced it with a full glass.

Later that evening, Big Joe noticed that her voice was getting louder by the minute. She'd been up on the dance floor, dancing by herself and imitating the strippers' moves while flirting with the men seated nearby.

Collapsing on a stool back at the bar, she was now talking non-stop and slurring her words. Drunk.

"Well, who knowsh," she yelled over the music at the bartender. "Might be schticking around thish dump anyway. My ex and I are workin' things out!"

"Oh yeah?" The bartender caught Big Joe's eye in a silent appeal.

"Maybe you know'im? Jimmy Barnes!" The canned music ended just as she yelled out Jim's name. Several heads turned her way.

She looked back at the crowd behind her. "Maybe somebuddy here knowsh him? Jimmy Barnes? My ever-lovin' husband?"

Big Joe was beside her in a moment.

"Look honey, I think you've had enough," he cautioned. The woman twisted her fingers into the sleeve of his T-shirt.

"Aw, come on, baby…the party's jus' gettin' going!"

Big Joe took her by the arm and quickly escorted her to the door. She lurched side to side as she went.

"Stand there. I'm calling you a taxi," he ordered.

She hung on his arm, a provocative expression on her face.

"Aw, lemme stay…I can make it worth your while, baby," she cajoled, putting her hand on his belt and starting to undo it.

Big Joe pushed her hand away. "Stop that!" he commanded.

The woman put on her best pout.

"I'm gonna tell my Jimmy on you!" she whimpered, then laughed loudly.

Big Joe took her outside when the taxi finally showed up.

* * *

Nora was getting her hair trimmed at the Clip and Curl late the next morning. As usual, Dory Berholtz was filling her in on the latest Harmony gossip.

"Say, did you hear about the ruckus at The Wobbly Dog last night? You'll love it! Some woman was in there getting hammered and yelling her head off! Told everyone she was Jim Barnes' wife!"

Nora's stomach dropped. "Oh, really?" She feigned disinterest.

"I guess she was dancing around, drunk as a lord and claiming that she and Jim were getting back together."

Nora swallowed hard, fearing that she may be sick. She didn't want to hear more.

Dory continued. "He seems like such a nice guy. I met him at the Grand Opening of his store. Who knew he had a wife like that? That poor little girl," Dory remarked as she finished trimming.

"Are you sure that's who it was? His wife?" Nora asked.

"Sure as sure. Big Joe was in earlier for a haircut. He told me he had to throw her out," Dory answered.

Nora sat silent as Dory finished styling her hair, then went up front to pay.

"Thanks, Dory," she said.

"Anytime." Dory gave her change and Nora went out into the street.

She walked a few feet then stopped and leaned against a wall for a moment. Then she continued to her car and drove slowly home. She entered her house and Henry greeted her enthusiastically. She patted his head absentmindedly.

Nora made her way to the kitchen and brewed a cup of tea. She sat down at the kitchen table and took a sip.

Then she put her head down on her arms and sobbed.

CHAPTER THIRTEEN

Jim and Glenna followed the waiter to a back table in Pasta Italia and settled themselves in. They had been looking at the menu for a few minutes when Rachelle arrived and joined them. She was wearing a tight neon pink tank top, shiny silver metallic leggings and pink sandals with six inch heels. *Still the same style sense. Some things never change*, Jim reflected.

"Hello, honey!" Rachelle leaned over to give Glenna a kiss, but Glenna shrank back.

Jim shook his head. His daughter was still wary and no doubt could smell the alcohol and cigarettes on Rachelle's breath. For a moment Rachelle looked angry, then quickly replaced her frown with a wide smile that didn't soften the brittle coldness in her eyes.

"Hey, Jimmy. How are you?"

"Fine."

Rachelle sat down and opened her menu. "I'm starved! Do you come here a lot? What do you recommend?"

Jim and Glenna looked at each other.

"We usually have pepperoni mushroom pizza," Glenna answered.

"Pepperoni mushroom it is! Extra large!" Rachelle put her menu down and looked over her shoulder. "Where's that waiter?"

Jim waved the waiter over to the table. Rachelle ordered the pizza, and asked them what they wanted to drink. *As if she's planning to pay*, Jim thought.

Glenna ordered a lemonade and Jim a beer. Rachelle ordered a double vodka rocks.

"So, here we are, just like old times." Rachelle smiled brightly at Jim and Glenna, who both gazed back at her stone-faced.

"Don't get carried away, Rachelle," Jim responded. "This is a meeting so Glenna can get to know you."

The waiter brought their drinks and Jim took a long sip of his beer. Glenna stirred her lemonade slowly, watching the straw go round and round in her glass.

Rachelle took a big swallow of her vodka rocks. "Of course. Baby girl, you sure grew up nice."

"Thank you," Glenna muttered, still staring at her drink.

An awkward silence followed.

Rachelle leaned forward. "So tell me, what grade are you in?"

Glenna looked at her father, who nodded. "Grade six."

"Almost in Junior High! Wow! Pretty soon it will all be about boys, boys, boys!"

Glenna frowned. "I don't think so," she said. "I want to concentrate on my studies. I want to go to university someday."

Rachelle laughed a bit too loudly. "Oh, you say that now, but you'll change your mind! I was one of the most popular girls in Junior High. You'll be the same."

Rachelle turned her attention to Jim before Glenna could respond. "So, the business going well?"

Jim set down his glass. "Yes, pretty well. We had a Grand Opening and we had a good response. Not much competition in this market."

"Why'd you move out here, Jimmy? It's a one-horse town with not much going for it as far as I can see. Wouldn't Glenna have been better off in Calgary?"

Jim gritted his teeth. "We like it here," he answered.

"That's right, we like it." Glenna came quickly to her father's defense.

"Well, different strokes as they say." Rachelle had already downed her first vodka and had ordered another.

"What are your plans, Rachelle?" Jim was hoping to hear that she would be moving on, sooner rather than later.

"Oh…I don't know. Maybe I'll stick around for a while. Do you know of any cheap rentals here? I'm staying in the Vista Motel at the moment."

"No," Jim said with conviction, and left it at that.

Glenna was staring at her glass again. She looked up at Rachelle. "Why did you leave?" she asked, her voice breaking a little.

"Why, I had to, honey," Rachelle answered, as if it were the most natural thing in the world. "Some bad luck came my way, and I figured it was best to deal with it on my own instead of involving you or your dad." Jim threw Rachelle a warning look.

"What happened?" Glenna pressed.

"There was a misunderstanding. I got accused of some stuff I didn't do, so I had to be on the down-low for a while."

"What's the down-low?" Glenna's brow was furrowed.

"Keeping my head down, you know, staying away from more trouble."

The pizza arrived, and for a few minutes they concentrated on their food. Jim was grateful for the break in conversation.

"How come you were gone for so long?" Glenna asked as she finished off her first piece of pizza.

Rachelle took a moment to answer. *Thinking up excuses*, thought Jim.

"Well, I thought I'd give you and your dad a chance to be on your own until it was the right time to come back."

Really? Jim thought. He wondered whether he should tell Glenna then and there that Rachelle had been locked up for eight years. It wasn't the right place or time, but he couldn't stand hearing Rachelle make excuses. Still, in the end, he had to let Glenna judge for herself.

He saw a defiant look come over Rachelle's face. "I'd like to see more of Glenna," she asserted. "I phoned and talked to a lawyer yesterday about arranging that."

Jim felt the color drain from his face. Glenna looked panicked and her eyes pleaded with him across the table.

"You and I will discuss that later," he stated with a deadly calm he didn't feel.

"Okey dokey!" Rachelle seemed unconcerned. She stuffed another piece of pizza in her mouth. He noticed that Glenna had stopped eating after Rachelle had mentioned the lawyer. Rachelle turned to Glenna again. "So, tell me what you've been up to, Baby."

Cautiously, Glenna shared a few details about her new life in Harmony and mentioned that she was enjoying the soccer league.

"Sports are always good. Got lots of friends?" Rachelle inquired.

Glenna nodded. "I have one or two new friends. That's all you really need."

"Oh, I don't know, the more friends the better I say! A bunch of friends means you've always got people to help you when the chips are down. I've had to rely on a lot of people to keep me going." Rachelle was wiping her fingers on her napkin and gesturing with her glass for yet another refill.

I bet, Jim thought. *More like you've used a lot of people to take care of your needs.*

"Jimmy, I'd like to see Glenna on my own this week. Maybe for lunch?"

Jim looked over at Glenna. Glenna, not sure how to react, stared back, her eyes filled with fear.

"Well, we'll see. Glenna and I will talk about it when we get home and give you a call," Jim answered.

"Dammit, Jimmy, cut me some slack!" Rachelle's demeanor suddenly changed. Her voice was edgy and harsh. "She's my kid, too! I did all the hard work to bring her into this world, and I have my rights!" Drinking three vodkas had brought out her belligerent side.

Glenna's head was down and her face was red. Jim could tell she was holding back tears with difficulty. He waved the waiter over. "The check, please."

After paying, Jim turned to Rachelle.

"We'd better be going. We'll talk on the phone, Rachelle."

He pulled out Glenna's chair.

"Goodbye," Glenna said quietly, one tear rolling down her cheek.

"Goodbye, Baby Doll! I'll look forward to our lunch together!" Rachelle waved to the waiter to bring her yet another drink.

Jim seethed. *Lunch? Over my dead body.* He handed Glenna his handkerchief as they left the restaurant.

* * *

"Nora?"

"Yes?"

Thank God. He had been trying to reach her all week, but all he got was the answering machine.

"It's me, Jim."

Her voice was hesitate. "Yes...?"

"Nora, we need to talk." He held his breath, waiting for her reply.

"I don't know. I don't think it's a good idea." She sounded doubtful.

He blew out his breath. "Nora, please, just listen to what I have to say."

"Jim, I've been hearing things around town about your ex. I really don't want to get involved."

"It's not what you think, Nora, I can guarantee you that." No doubt the whole town was speculating about Rachelle.

"All I know is what I've heard, Jim. That your ex is in town and you are planning to reconcile with her. What am I supposed to think? It's better if I stay completely out of it."

"Nora, no!" He hated small town gossips. "You have to give me a chance to explain. Please!"

"Goodbye, Jim."

Jim hung up the phone and stood staring out his office window.

* * *

Early Sunday morning, after visiting the manager's office at the Vista Motel, Jim knocked at the door of Number Nine.

Rachelle opened it with the chain still on. She was dressed in a man's T-shirt and nothing else. She quickly looked over her shoulder. Jim could hear the shower going.

"Oh hi, Jimmy! What can I do you for?"

"I need to talk to you, Rachelle." Jim could hear a male voice singing in the shower.

"Just a minute, Jimmy. Let's get a coffee at the motel cafe. I'll be right out." She shut the door briefly and reappeared after a few minutes. "Okay, let's go."

"Sorry if I disturbed you at a bad time," Jim said, sarcasm tinging his voice.

Rachelle cast him a hard look. "Oh, chill out, Jimmy. A girl's got her needs, after all."

"Sure he can manage to get ready without you?"

"He'll be just fine."

They entered the coffee shop and sat down. A frowsy, tired-looking waitress took their order and brought back two black coffees.

Rachelle took two pills out of her purse and washed them down with the coffee. "So, what is it?"

Jim got right to the point. "What have you been saying around town, Rachelle?"

"Nothing. What do you mean?" Rachelle was avoiding eye contact.

"I heard you were telling people we were getting back together."

She rolled her eyes. "Would I do that? You know how small towns are, it's all gossip. Besides, would that be a bad thing, the two of us getting together? I remember you were quite a tiger in the sack before things went wrong." Rachelle reached under the table and squeezed his knee with her hand. "I could handle some more of that, you sexy beast! It's been a long time," she said with a lascivious grin.

Jim angrily pushed her hand away. "Quit it! There's no way that's ever going to happen, Rachelle. What if Glenna heard the gossip? How would I explain that to her?"

Rachelle picked up the sugar dispenser and poured a waterfall of sugar into her coffee. "Whatever. I told you I wanted to see more of Glenna and I intend to."

"No way." Jim's tone was firm.

Rachelle stirred her coffee and raised an eyebrow. "There is a way, if you just listen, Jimmy."

Jim shook his head. "No. I don't want you in Glenna's life, Rachelle, get that straight."

"Okay then, how about this? I'll step right out of her life…and never return…for a price."

Jim set his cup down. "What?"

Rachelle leaned forward and locked her eyes to his. "Look, you're making good money and soon you'll be making even more. What if you just sent me some money every month, so I could get a new start? I could skip town and leave you both alone."

Jim stared at her. "That's blackmail, Rachelle. Why should I give you anything? Forget it."

Rachelle sat back again. "Well, then, I guess we'll just have to see what happens. I'm pretty broke since I got out, which is why I'm staying at this dump. I need money, Jimmy and I need it now."

"You're not getting a penny out of me, Rachelle!"

"Well, maybe I'll just contact that custody lawyer again," Rachelle mused.

"That's crap and you know it." Jim's voice was raised. An older couple at the next table looked up from their bacon and eggs. "No judge will grant you even partial custody of Glenna."

Rachelle finished her coffee and looked thoughtful. "Maybe." Jim could see she was thinking up a new tactic. What she said next froze his blood. "You wouldn't want anything bad to happen to her, would you? It's easy for someone to have an accident or disappear up here in the mountains."

Jim slammed his hand down on the table. All the customers and staff looked up this time, startled. "Don't you dare threaten us, Rachelle! I'm warning you. I want you out of Harmony today! I mean it!"

Rachelle glared at him. "I was once your wife, and you owe me! I'm not finished yet by a long shot!"

Jim was yelling now. "Get out of Harmony! And stay out! Leave us alone!"

The manager was heading their way. Rachelle got up and smiled sweetly at him. "Coffee's on you, I guess." She turned and went out the door.

CHAPTER FOURTEEN

Nora found herself missing Jim's phone calls. Life seemed so dull and lifeless and...depressing since she had heard about Rachelle being back in town.

She hated how their last phone conversation went, but what else could she do? If his ex-wife said they were reconciling, she had to assume there was something to it. Why would the woman lie?

Henry woofed to remind her it was time to feed him. Nora filled his bowl and set it on the kitchen floor. She watched him gobble up his kibble.

It was clear that Jim's ex had problems. He didn't strike her as the type to be tolerant of a woman who drank and carried on. Maybe there was more to the story than she had heard. Should she find out? Or would she be getting into a situation that was way over her head?

She thought of Glenna. Jim was a good man and cared deeply for his daughter. She'd been pretty abrupt with him. Maybe he deserved a second hearing. She picked up the phone and dialed, but got the answering machine. She decided to try anyway.

"Jim, it's Nora. I just wanted to say...maybe I should have heard you out the other day. I don't know what's going on but I want to be a friend to you and Glenna. Anyway, give me a call when you have time. Bye."

She hung up the phone and hoped she'd done the right thing.

* * *

Coming back from his meeting with Rachelle, Jim could barely contain his rage. He gripped the steering wheel tightly. Once home, he parked in his driveway and sat in the car, thinking about what Rachelle had said. He knew she was capable of the worst kind of behavior. What if he'd put himself or Glenna in jeopardy? Should he have agreed to Rachelle's terms, just to get her out of the picture and keep Glenna safe?

No. He had made the right decision. He wasn't giving in to threats. Rachelle was a bully and a liar. Once she realized she couldn't get money out of him, she would go elsewhere to find new targets. That's what he had to count on.

Glenna was in the kitchen, scrambling eggs in the frying pan. She popped two slices of bread in the toaster and looked up as he came in. "Dad? Where have you been?" She cracked another egg and tossed it in. "I'm making us breakfast."

"Just out. Thanks, Honey. I'd love some breakfast."

The toast popped and Glenna buttered both pieces, giving one to him and putting one on her plate. Then she doled out the eggs and they both sat down to eat.

Jim knew he had to explain about Rachelle. "Glenna, I need to talk to you. I've just been to see your mother."

Glenna looked nervous. "And?"

"I've asked her to leave town and leave us alone."

Glenna heaved a sigh of relief. "Oh, Dad, I'm so glad."

"Are you, Sweetie?"

Glenna nodded as she took a bite of toast. "I don't like her. She makes me uncomfortable, and I smelled booze on her breath in the restaurant the other night. Did you notice how much she was drinking?"

"I did. Glenna, I didn't want to tell you this but I feel you are old enough now to handle it. Your mother wasn't just away." He took a deep breath. "She was in prison."

Glenna's fork stopped halfway to her mouth. She stared at her father.

"Prison?"

"That's right."

"What for?"

"That doesn't matter. What matters is that she doesn't belong in our lives, now or ever."

Glenna put her fork down and processed this new information. "Do you think she ever loved me?" Her eyes were beseeching.

Jim put his hand on hers. "Honey, I honestly don't know. I wish I could tell you that she did."

Glenna thought for a few moments. "So, is she leaving?"

"Yes, I hope so."

"What if she doesn't?"

Jim patted her hand. "We'll take this a day at a time, Sprout." He hoped his words were reassuring, but they seemed so inadequate.

"What if the other kids find out my mom was in prison?" Glenna's face wore a horrified expression as she considered the ramifications.

"They won't find out." Jim promised her. "I'll see to that."

Glenna got up, walked around to his chair and hugged him. "Dad, I feel scared. I don't like her and I don't want to see her. I was afraid you'd let her stay."

"Don't worry. I was clear with her. I love you so much, Glenna, and I'm going to make sure everything turns out all right."

"I love you too, Daddy."

After breakfast Glenna went off to soccer practice. Jim checked his messages before heading to the store. Hearing Nora's message, he knew he had to see her. Right away.

* * *

Henry heard the doorbell and raced to the front of the house, jumping around with excitement as Nora opened the door. Jim was standing there with his hands in his pockets.

"Jim?"

"Hi, Nora. I hope you don't mind me stopping by." Henry jumped up on Jim, his tail wagging wildly.

Nora took hold of Henry's collar. "Henry! Get down! Um…no, I don't mind. Come in. Would you like a cup of coffee?"

"Coffee would be great. May I use your phone to tell Nick I'll be a bit late coming to work?"

"Of course."

After a quick phone call to the store, Jim sat down at the kitchen table, where Nora had already poured coffee for both of them. She put the cream and sugar where Jim could reach them.

"Nora, I got your phone message. Thank you for calling."

"You're welcome, Jim. I've missed you." Nora poured some cream in her coffee.

"I've missed you too. Can we talk?"

Nora nodded. "Yes. I want to understand."

Jim stared into his coffee. Nora waited patiently for him to find his words.

"Nora, my divorce wasn't like some other divorces. I met a woman I thought I loved, but she turned out to be someone completely different. Rachelle has some serious problems."

Nora leaned back in her chair. "It happens sometimes."

"Yes…well, after Glenna was born, Rachelle went completely off the rails. I spent a lot of time retrieving her from bars and motels. She'd go off for days at a time. I pretty much had to care for Glenna by myself. I'm not saying that to make you feel sorry for me, it's just a fact."

Nora reached across the table and laid her hand on his. "I'm so sorry you had to go through that."

Jim took a few deep breaths. "It just got worse and worse, until…I had a call from the police. I thought she might be dead, but she'd been arrested."

"Oh God, Jim."

Jim's face reddened. "It was serious. A serious offence. Nora, she's been in prison these last eight years. And now she's back. She said she wanted to get to know her daughter, but she's really after my money, as it turns out."

"Does Glenna know? Is she okay?" Nora asked.

"She's okay. Glenna met Rachelle a couple times, but doesn't like her. I only told Glenna this morning about her mother being in prison. That was tough, but I figured she could handle it." Nora heard the doubt in his voice. She remained silent but pressed Jim's hand.

He looked up at her. "Rachelle's threatened Glenna. And she wants to blackmail me. She says she'll stay away from us for a price."

He could see the silent question in Nora's eyes, and answered it.

"I didn't give in, of course. I told her to leave town and leave us alone. Please don't judge us by what you hear about Rachelle," he pleaded. "Glenna and I have made a new life for ourselves. We agree that we want nothing to do with her. I'm praying that she'll leave town and that's the last we'll hear of her."

Nora squeezed his hand again. "I sure hope it will work out, Jim. You let Rachelle know how you feel and stood your ground. You did the best you could do under the circumstances."

Jim gently clasped her fingers. "Nora, you are the best thing that has happened to me in a long time." He lifted her hand up and kissed her palm. "Please give me another chance," he pleaded.

Nora couldn't help herself. She stood up slightly in her chair, leaned over and kissed him on the lips. "I'm so happy I met you, Jim Barnes. We won't let this stop us."

A deep gladness flowed through him. He stood up and drew her to him. "Thank you," he said simply, then kissed her tenderly and held her for a long, long time.

CHAPTER FIFTEEN

The following Saturday, Jim and Glenna were having breakfast. Another bright and sunny day. The weatherman had predicted the same for Sunday.

"How do you feel about going on a picnic tomorrow, Sprout?"

"Dad, that would be awesome! Can I make all the food?"

"Of course, make anything you want. Oh, and Nora is coming with us. I think Henry, too. We thought we'd go out to Banff Park."

Glenna was beside herself with excitement. "Really? I'll make egg salad sandwiches, and ham sandwiches, and …"

Jim laughed. He enjoyed seeing Glenna so happy after the stresses of the last week.

"Hang on there! Maybe you should get in touch with Nora and plan it with her. I'll buy a watermelon and some chips and sodas."

Glenna clapped her hands. "Okay. I'll call Nora this morning!"

* * *

Nora hummed as she mixed up an angel food cake batter. Before leaving her house on Sunday morning, Jim had suggested they take Glenna on a picnic the following weekend to help them forget the troubles they'd had with

Rachelle. Nora loved the idea. A getaway for the three of them would help get things back to normal. What could be better? She told Jim about a great picnic spot she knew in Banff Park that had firewood, toilets and a water tap.

The phone rang. Nora wiped her hands on a tea towel and picked it up.

"Hey, Nora, it's me, Glenna! Dad told me about the picnic!"

"I'm so glad. It should be a lot of fun. I'm going to bring Henry's leash so he can walk with us."

"I want to make egg salad sandwiches and ham sandwiches. And we've got cookies. And Dad's getting a watermelon," Glenna said.

Nora smiled to herself. "Great, I'm making an angel food cake with whipped cream and fresh strawberries."

"Yay! That sounds yummy. What are you going to wear?"

"Just my shorts and a T-shirt and runners. You?" Nora reached across to the fridge with her free hand, opened the door and pulled out a basket of strawberries.

"The same. And we should bring hats - there's ticks in the woods, Dad said."

"That's a very smart idea. I'll bring my baseball hat."

"So we'll see you tomorrow morning?"

Nora put the strawberries under running water in the sink. "Yes you will! Have a great day, Glenna."

"You too, Nora. Pet Henry for me."

"I will."

"Bye!"

"Bye!"

Nora hung up the phone and reached down to pet Henry. "How lucky are we, Henry, to be going out tomorrow with two of our favorite people in Harmony?"

Henry gave a short sharp bark and wagged his tail. He clearly approved.

* * *

On Sunday morning, Jim and Glenna drove over to pick up Nora and Henry. All were in high spirits as they left Harmony and chatted happily until they got to the park gates. Jim had a parks sticker on the truck so they breezed through the gates and headed for the picnic area Nora had suggested.

Jim checked his rear view mirror. The traffic was busy today, not surprising for a Sunday around Banff. He noticed a red Corolla not far behind as they wound their way into the park. Those people seemed to be going to the same area. Picnicking, probably.

"Look, Dad, an elk!" Glenna pointed at the side of the highway. Several cars had stopped to view the elk grazing nearby. Jim pulled over briefly and then they set off again.

In twenty minutes they arrived at the trailhead leading to the picnic site. Nora explained they would have a short hike in to reach the site. They decided to leave the food secured in the truck until it was time to eat.

"The good thing about this spot is that few people want to bother walking in," Nora explained. "So it tends to be very quiet."

It took only a few minutes to reach their destination. It was quiet, as Nora predicted. They had the place to themselves.

"Shall we go for a walk first?" Jim suggested. *Coming out here was a great idea*, he thought, as he observed the happiness glowing in his daughter's face.

"Oh yes, Dad! Let's!"

Jim and Nora exchanged a smile. They headed down one of the side trails, Henry on his leash. Glenna collected pinecones and Henry found a small creek to splash in. Glenna laughed at his antics and used her phone to take a few photos. After about half an hour, they retraced their steps back to the site. Nora pulled a longer leash from her bag and tied Henry to a tree. He could still move around freely but was restricted to the picnic area. Nora didn't want him bothering any wildlife.

She pulled out a waxed cloth and draped it on the picnic table, then used clips to fasten it in place while Jim and Glenna went back to the truck to get the food.

Henry barked excitedly when he saw them returning with the coolers. Glenna put the pinecones she'd collected on the table for decoration and then set out plates of sandwiches covered with nets to keep the insects off. Jim opened the sodas and broke out the chips.

"This is awesome!" Glenna said, munching on a chip. Henry lay at her feet, staring intently at the chip in her hand. "Not for you, Henry! Here, I have a dog cookie for you that Nora gave me." Henry ate his cookie with relish.

They tucked into the sandwiches, cookies and cake with gusto. Jim, now feeling very relaxed, cut generous pieces of watermelon for everyone.

"I'm so full!" Nora laughed, patting her stomach. "I ate way more than I should!"

Jim smiled. "That's what picnics are for," he joked. He loved to hear her laugh. He went back to the truck and retrieved the small axe he'd brought to split some kindling for a fire. Nora reached for her camping kettle to make tea and asked Glenna to fill it at the tap. Soon the kettle was steaming away and Nora set out the cups, milk and sugar.

"Want some tea, Glenna?" Jim called.

"No thanks, Dad. Can I go and take some more pictures on my phone? I think it would be nice to look at them later and remember our picnic."

"Sure, Sprout, just don't wander too far."

"Okay, I promise. Can Henry come?"

Nora shook her head. "No, Sweetie, I think it's better he stays with us. You'd have a hard time holding him and taking pictures too."

"Okay. See you soon!"

"Remember, don't go far," Jim reminded her. He knew he could trust Glenna's judgement, but he was naturally cautious when it came to his girl.

"Yes, Dad!" Glenna called over her shoulder as she headed down one of the trails.

* * *

Alone at the site, Jim took the opportunity to sit beside Nora and put his arm around her waist. They sat that way for a long time, sipping their tea. Jim couldn't remember when he'd been so content. "I hope Glenna won't wander too far," he said.

"I'm sure she'll be fine," said Nora. "She's a sensible girl."

Jim reached up and ran his fingers through Nora's long luxuriant hair. She leaned her head back and closed her eyes as his index finger traced around her ear and down her throat. He leaned in and began kissing her ear, moving down to her throat and pulling her closer to him. Nora turned her head and they kissed deeply for several minutes.

"Whew! You sure know how to get a man hot and bothered!" Jim whispered in her ear.

"I'm pretty distracted myself." Nora chuckled.

"I'm more than distracted!" he said, and kissed her again just as passionately.

Henry seemed oblivious to all this activity, having fallen asleep by a tree. Jim spread a blanket out on the grass near the table. Henry looked up briefly then put his head back down and closed his eyes.

Jim pulled Nora down onto the blanket and they lay on their sides about a foot apart, looking at each other. He stroked Nora's face and she put a hand on his arm.

"Such strong arms," she whispered and smiled. "It's plain to see you haven't spent your time pushing papers for a living."

Jim loved the feel of her fingers on his skin. "I can't believe we're here," he said softly. "I never thought I would be with a woman again."

Nora moved her hand up to his face and he pulled her closer.

"Jim…" she whispered his name. Then they were in each other's arms, kissing wildly, curling their legs around each other and pressing their bodies tightly together.

Finally, breathless, they pulled apart.

"We'd better cool this down before Glenna gets back," Jim cautioned.

Nora grinned playfully. "I guess so. It's hard to stop, though, isn't it?"

Jim rolled on his back and exhaled loudly. "You can say that again! I don't want to stop. I never want to stop. But we'd better all the same." He leaned up on one elbow and looked down at her.

"Nora Fitzgerald, you have cast a spell on me. Oh, don't look so innocent. I know what you're capable of.

How do I know you won't vanish suddenly into the forest with the other fey folk?"

Nora laughed and slapped him playfully. "I'm not going anywhere, Jim Barnes. Fey or not, why would I leave behind such a handsome and sexy man?" She sat up and looked around.

"Now, where's Glenna got to?" she asked.

Jim check his watch. "She should be back by now." He stood up, looked around and walked over to the trail Glenna had taken.

"Glenna?" he called out. "Time to come back! Glenna?"

His calls were met with silence.

CHAPTER SIXTEEN

In the next hour, they searched everywhere, calling loudly as they went. They took Henry with them in case he could pick up her scent. There were so many side trails she could have taken. It was already late in the afternoon. Finally, they returned to the picnic site for a drink.

"Where on earth did she go?" Jim looked at Nora and they saw the fear in each other's eyes.

"Jim, I think we need some help," she offered.

Jim drank his water and sat silently, considering his next move. "Look, you stay here with Henry, in case she comes back. You've got lots of food and water. I'm going to drive back to Harmony and get help. I'll stop at the gates to let the wardens know. Maybe they'll have some suggestions."

Nora nodded miserably. She knew Jim was beside himself with worry, so she'd do as he asked and stay put until help came. "I agree. That's a good idea. I'm sure we'll find her."

Jim looked at her, his face drawn. He seemed to have aged ten years in the last hour. "I'll be back." He jumped in the truck and drove off. Henry, sensing something was amiss, howled mournfully.

* * *

Nora sat down and let a few tears fall, now that Jim had left. My God, it was only their first outing together!

All Jim had wanted to do was relax and forget his troubles. Why did this have to happen now?

Brought up in Harmony, Nora knew well the mishaps that could befall someone in the mountains. She couldn't bear the idea of Glenna facing the coming night alone and afraid. In the past, Nora had helped search for visitors who had been lost in the park. A bad trip or fall and Glenna could be in real trouble if they didn't find her quickly. It got so cold at night in the mountains, even in the summer. She was glad that Jim was letting the wardens know. They would be a great help.

Pull yourself together, Nora! She stood up, went over to the tap and splashed some cold water on her face. She had always been good in an emergency. She had to think clearly and stay ready.

* * *

Jim drove like a demon back to the gates. He quickly let the park warden know what had happened and got her to radio for assistance. He explained that he was going to Harmony to notify the police and would be back to meet the wardens at the picnic site.

Another high-speed drive got him back to Harmony, where he went directly to the RCMP post. The Mounties wasted no time. They leashed their search dog and several officers packed up the rescue gear. For Jim, every minute of this was an eternity. As instructed, he rushed home to get a piece of Glenna's clothing for the dog to sniff. He knew this was important but hated wasting the time. Grabbing one of Glenna's T-shirts, he raced back to meet the Mounties.

* * *

Nora gave Henry a bowl of water and watched him lap it up. Jim had been gone a long time. Or, at least it seemed that he had.

"Where is Glenna, Henry? Where could she have wandered to?" *She's a smart girl,* Nora thought. Maybe she knew enough to stay put until help came. *Please let her stay put.* She walked back over to the picnic table and sat down.

Suddenly Henry began barking furiously with a strange yelp in his bark she had never heard before. Nora turned and saw a blonde woman standing by the trail leading into the site.

Nora was confused. Was this a searcher sent from town?

The woman spoke, her voice harsh.

"Well, well. If it isn't Jimmy's new flame!"

She wore tight jeans and a red tank-top under a jean jacket. Her cropped hair was sticking out in several directions. She was carrying a large purse and wearing high-heeled boots.

Nora had never seen Henry so agitated. Still tied to the tree, he was barking frantically at the woman and pulling hard on his leash.

"Who are you?" Nora asked.

"Why, I'm your worst nightmare, honey!" The woman laughed and pulled something out of her purse.

Was that a gun?

It was.

And the woman was pointing it at her.

Nora froze, but managed to speak. "What do you want?"

"I want you to come with me." The woman was smiling, but her eyes were ice cold.

"I...I...can't!" Nora spit out. "We've lost a little girl, and I need to wait for her here."

The woman laughed loudly. "Oh you have, have you? Well, I think you'd better consider saving your own skin right at the moment." She waved the gun toward the road.

"March!" she commanded. Henry growled and leapt toward her but couldn't reach her.

"Easy, Henry." Nora said to her dog. Reluctantly, she began to walk up the trail, the woman a few paces behind her. *What was happening? Could this get any worse? What would Jim think when he found her gone?*

Jim. Suddenly she knew who this woman was.

"You're Rachelle." Nora stopped walking and turned toward her.

Rachelle raised an eyebrow. "Bravo. It took you awhile, but you finally figured it out. Keep walking!" Rachelle waved the gun toward the road again. In a few minutes, Nora could see a red Corolla parked at the trailhead.

"Why are you doing this?" she asked.

"Never mind why, just do what I say."

Coming up to the car, Nora could hear a thumping sound. Rachelle banged the gun on the trunk. "Quiet in there, dammit!"

"Who's in there? Is it Glenna?" Nora asked, horrified.

Without answering, Rachelle opened the back door of the Corolla. She pulled out some duct tape and tore off a long strip. "Come over here!"

Nora obeyed and Rachelle slapped a piece of duct tape over her mouth. "Now get in the back of the car and lie on the floor, face down! Put your hands behind your back!"

Nora had no choice but to do as she was told. Her mind worked a million miles a minute. If that was Glenna in the trunk, how could she save her? *Stay Calm. Think.* Rachelle taped Nora's wrists behind her back and then bound her ankles. Nora could feel a blanket being thrown over her. It smelled like cigarettes.

"Now be quiet, or I'll make you and the kid wish you had never met me."

I already wish that, thought Nora. *Oh how I wish it!* So it was Glenna in the trunk. She had to keep her cool. *Stay strong, Glenna*, she urged silently. It was now dusk.

As Rachelle drove off, Nora tried to determine what direction the car was travelling. It seemed to be going back toward Harmony. Maybe the warden at the gates would stop them. But she couldn't tell where they were in relation to the gates. The car drove on and on.

Soon they were pulling off the highway. It was getting very dark. She lifted her head and could see a neon sign flashing in the window but couldn't read it.

Rachelle got out. Nora could hear a key opening a door, then heard her captor walk around to the back door of the Corolla.

Opening the door, Rachelle leaned in and whispered. "Now listen to me! We're at a motel. I'm going to undo your ankles and when I say so, you'll get out of the car and walk straight through the door of the motel room. I'll be right behind you. Don't try to attract attention or believe me, I'll cut that kid's throat right in front of you!" She showed Nora a large butcher knife and then used it to cut the tape around Nora's ankles. Nora saw her straighten up and look around.

"Okay…now!"

Nora sat up and swung her feet out onto the pavement. She could see the neon sign now. *Vista Motel.* Pulling herself up, she walked quickly around the back of the car and into the motel room. She could feel Rachelle behind her pushing the point of the knife against her ribs.

"Sit down on the bed! And don't move!"

Rachelle returned to the car and unlocked the trunk. She reached in and seemed to be using the knife. Nora heard her whispering again. "Now you're going to get out and go in the door of the motel room." She saw Rachelle help Glenna out of the trunk.

"Hurry up!" Rachelle roughly pushed Glenna through the door and onto the bed next to Nora, then turned and closed the door behind her.

Glenna looked at Nora. Her face was red and puffy from crying and she had dirty streaks down her cheeks. Her eyes were wide, terrified. Nora looked at her with soft eyes, trying to silently comfort her. Rachelle rearranged them on the bed so they were lying with their backs to each other, and re-taped their ankles. She walked over to the dresser, poured herself a large glass of whiskey from the bottle that was sitting there, and sat down in the chair facing the end of the bed. She lit a cigarette.

"So, here we all are, one big not-so-happy family." She cackled, raising her drink in a mocking toast. "Well, I guess Jimmy will have to re-think paying me off after all. I figure he'll cough up plenty to get you two back."

* * *

Nora woke after dreaming that she was paralyzed under water. Her heart beat like a hammer. For a few minutes she thought the dream was reality, as she struggled to breathe through her nose. Then she remembered. She was in a motel room, bound and gagged along with Glenna. Under the control of a madwoman.

The rays of morning sun seeped through the blinds. She could feel the warmth of Glenna's body behind her on the bed. She lifted her head and saw Rachelle asleep in the chair, the near-empty whiskey bottle beside her on the dresser.

Slowly, Nora rolled over and gently nudged Glenna. The girl woke with a start and re-positioned herself so that she and Nora were face to face. Glenna whimpered behind the duct tape. Nora shook her head, nodded toward Rachelle, and then looked Glenna in the eyes. She tilted her chin to indicate Glenna, then tucked her chin to indicate herself. She twisted her head and nodded toward the door.

Glenna understood and nodded back. They both looked toward Rachelle. Nora closed her eyes and let her head fall, indicating that Glenna should pretend to sleep. Glenna put her head down and closed her eyes. Nora rolled onto her back, looked at the ceiling and waited.

As the sun got brighter, Rachelle began to stir. She rubbed her head and eyes and went into the bathroom. Nora watched her movements through nearly closed eyes, pretending to be asleep. Rachelle returned and stood over the bed before moving to the desk near the window where she pulled out some stationery and sat down to write. After a few minutes, she stuck a note in her pocket, then walked back to the bed. She shoved Nora roughly and Nora pretended to wake up.

Rachelle was on her knees by the bed, looking into Nora's face. She spoke quietly.

"Listen to me, bitch. I have some business to attend to. If you know what's good for you and her, you'll stay quiet until I get back. If I find you trying to escape when I return I'll kill both of you. I'll kill her in front of you and then slit your throat. Got it? I've got nothing to lose, believe me."

Nora nodded. Rachelle checked the tape on both of them and then moved to the door.

"I could be back in ten minutes, so don't try anything."

Nora nodded again. Rachelle opened the door and stepped out. She took a final look at her captives before closing and locking the door. Nora heard the car engine start and the crunch of tires on gravel. Immediately, she rolled back toward Glenna, who was now awake and looking at her with fear in her eyes. Nora nodded to her once more then rolled onto the floor.

* * *

There was no time to lose. Rachelle could be back at any minute. Nora hit the floor hard, but managed to protect her face. Using the bed as leverage, she got into a sitting position, then looked around the room. Something sharp, that's what she needed.

The whiskey bottle caught her eye. She slowly inched her way toward the dresser, scooting along on her butt and pulling with her legs. She turned around, put her bound hands behind her on the chair seat and lifted her body onto the chair.

Glenna watched her with wide eyes.

Nora knew it would be hard to grab the bottle. She managed to rise up in the chair, bracing herself against the chair back. She twisted her arms sideways and lifted them as high as she could. After several unsuccessful tries, she finally managed to grasp the bottle neck with her fingers.

Tired, she slumped back into the chair with her fingers holding the bottle behind her.

Now for the next phase. She eased her body back onto the floor and inched toward the bathroom, gripping the bottle tightly and dragging it behind her. She lined herself up beside the tub, swung her arms away and then brought the bottle crashing into the side of the tub with all the strength she had.

The bottle shattered. Whiskey and glass fragments sprayed across the floor. Nora sat and breathed deeply for several minutes. Carefully, she felt the floor behind her with her fingers until she found a glass fragment large enough to begin cutting the duct tape that bound her hands.

Her heart pounded. Every moment she expected Rachelle to walk back through the door. She could no longer see Glenna but knew Glenna was waiting for her.

Nora continued to push the glass against the tape until it began to tear. Once she had a sizeable tear she dropped the glass shard and pushed her hands hard against the tape. Nothing.

She felt around for the glass again, and started over.

Finally, she felt the tape begin to loosen. One final push and it broke. Her hands were free. She immediately tore the tape from her mouth and took a long breath. She shook out her hands which were half numb from being bound so long. Then she cut the tape around her ankles.

"Glenna?" Glenna was lying on the bed, looking up at her with pleading eyes.

Nora tore the tape off her mouth and Glenna took a gasping breath and started to cry.

"Nora! I'm so scared!"

"It's okay," Nora reassured her while cutting her free. "We're getting out of here, right now! Do you still have your phone?"

"She smashed it."

"Never mind," said Nora. "Let's get moving."

They cautiously opened the door a crack and scanned the parking lot and road.

Nora put her hand on Glenna's arm. "Let's go."

They ran first to the motel office and pounded on the door but no one came. Next they ran to the nearest motel doors and started knocking. At the second door a disheveled older man wearing striped pajamas opened the door. They could see a woman in bed behind him.

"Please help us!" Nora put arm around Glenna. "We've been held against our will in one of the other rooms and we need to contact the police."

"Honey…what is it?" The woman in the bed sounded sleepy.

The man stood staring at them, dumbfounded.

Nora tried again. "Please, there's no time to waste. Let us in! We need help. We have to call the police. Please!"

"Let them in, Arthur!" the woman called out.

The man stood aside and Nora and Glenna rushed in and shut the door behind them. Nora ran to the phone to dial 911. Glenna sat on the bed, sobbing quietly. The woman, now sitting up, put her arm around her.

"I'll drive you into town," the man offered. Nora nodded while explaining their situation to the dispatcher. "Yes, we've been held hostage overnight at the Vista Motel but managed to escape. You need to send someone right away because the woman who took us, Rachelle Barnes, may be back any time. She's armed. That's right. Room Nine."

Nora shook her head. "No, we're not staying here. One of the guests at the motel is driving us back into Harmony. Please contact Jim Barnes right away to let him know his daughter is safe. And hurry!"

Nora put the phone down and sat beside Glenna on the bed. Glenna leaned against her.

"My name's Flora Gibson," the woman said. "This is my husband, Arthur. What can we do?"

"Please," Nora urged, "we all should leave, right now! As I said, the woman who took us is armed, and she could be back any minute."

Flora and Arthur exchanged a glance and without another word Arthur rushed out, still in his pajamas, to start his car. Flora threw on a dressing gown and followed him with Nora and Glenna right behind her. They jumped into the car.

"Get going, Arthur!" Flora commanded.

Arthur pulled out onto the highway and floored it.

CHAPTER SEVENTEEN

For the first time in her life, Rachelle drove the speed limit on the highway. She couldn't afford to be stopped and questioned now. She'd seen a gas station up the highway about ten miles and her rental car needed gas. She also craved coffee and cigarettes. The gas station came in view. Rachelle drove in, filled the gas tank and walked into the station.

The young attendant behind the counter stood with the till open, counting his float. He closed the drawer when he saw Rachelle come in. Rachelle looked around. She was the only customer at that time in the morning. She approached the counter with a smile.

"Hi, honey, I'll have a pack of Player's and I'm gonna get a large coffee, plus the gas."

The attendant nodded and Rachelle went to get her coffee from the self-service dispenser. In the coffee area, she opened her purse and put her gun within reach, then walked back to the counter.

Just a kid, Rachelle thought. Tall and gangly with the vestiges of a moustache, he was wearing a black T-shirt with a heavy metal logo on the front. *No more than seventeen. Easy-peasy.* He looked up with a smile as he rang up Rachelle's purchases. She smiled back, looked around once again and pulled the gun from her purse.

"Keep smiling, sonny. We're gonna do this nice and slow. Just give me all the cash from the till. Put it in a plastic bag."

The boy stared at the gun. Then he raised his eyes to Rachelle.

"Wha..aat?" he said.

"The money from the till, idiot! Now! Unless you want a few holes in that nice T-shirt!"

The boy just stood there, gawking at her.

Freakin' kids, Rachelle thought. "Do you hear me? Do it now!"

The boy opened the till and slowly drew a plastic bag from underneath the counter. He started putting money into it.

"The change too?" he asked. His hands were shaking so violently he could hardly hold the bag.

"Of course the change too, fool! Just get on with it, and hurry up!"

Rachelle threw a look over her shoulder. The coast was still clear. "Now, throw a couple of cartons of Player's in there as well."

The boy squatted down and reached under the counter, pulling out the cartons of cigarettes.

Just then, the air hose bell sounded. They both jumped. Keeping her gun trained on the attendant, Rachelle looked over her shoulder.

It was the Mounties, filling up their car. Rachelle knew her body hid the gun in her hand, but she only had seconds to assess and control the situation. She had to think fast.

"Those are cops," she said to the attendant. "I'm going to put this gun in my jacket pocket, but I'm still pointing it at you. Don't say anything, and don't make any stupid moves, or I'll shoot your sorry ass after I've shot them. Just serve them and let them leave."

The boy nodded and handed her the bag. Rachelle stuffed it inside her jacket as one of the Mounties walked in to pay.

"Oh, I forgot something, honey. Just give me a minute." Rachelle headed to the back of the store and pretended to look at the merchandise.

The Mountie greeted the boy and handed him two twenties.

"Um…I'm sorry, they haven't brought me my new float," the boy explained, his voice cracking. His eyes shifted back and forth from the Mountie to the back of the store.

The Mountie glanced back toward Rachelle then smiled at the clerk, who was shaking like a leaf. "No problem, son," he said calmly. "Would it be okay if we came in later to pay? You know we're good for it!"

The boy laughed nervously.

"S..S..Sure, no problem." His voice was shaky.

"See you later, then!" The Mountie walked back out to the car, got in and drove away.

Rachelle walked back to the counter. "Good job," she said, "Now show me the back way out."

"Please don't hurt me," the boy pleaded.

"Quiet!" Rachelle snapped. "Just do what I say." Before she could get another word out, two Mounties charged through the front door, their guns drawn.

"Police! Freeze!" one of them yelled. Rachelle drew her gun out of her pocket, stepped behind the counter and pulled the boy in front of her. She pointed the gun at his head.

"Back off!" she screamed. "I'll kill him...I mean it!"

The Mounties lowered their guns and one of them put a hand up, palm out.

"Just cool down, lady. We don't want anyone to get hurt. Let the boy go."

"No way!" Rachelle jerked the boy closer to her. "Let me get to my car or he's gone."

The Mountie nodded. Rachelle pulled the boy from behind the counter and the Mounties stood aside as she marched her hostage out the door and toward the Corolla, watching the Mounties over her shoulder as she went. At the pumps, she opened the passenger side door and shoved the boy in, her gun still pointed at him. She closed the door and walked around to the driver's side, still watching the Mounties in the station.

Then, too late, she noticed a third Mountie crouched behind the police car parked nearby. A shot rang out. Rachelle's body slammed against the car as the bullet tore into her upper thigh. She sank down and started shooting toward the police car. She could hear a dog barking. The two Mounties ran out from the station toward her and she twisted to turn her fire on them. Two more shots rang out.

Then there was silence.

* * *

Back at the picnic site, Jim and Nick were waiting with the wardens for the Mounties to show up.

"Where are they?" Jim was angry. "They promised to start searching with us first thing this morning!" One of the wardens handed him a cup of coffee.

"They must have been called out to an incident," the warden explained. "There's only three Mounties in Harmony, so if something happened, they have to go. Hang in there, Jim. We'll start searching and take you with us. Nick, you wait here to let the Mounties know the plan once they arrive."

Nick nodded and Jim headed off down the trail with the wardens. Further down, the group split up to cover more of the side trails.

After an hour, Jim paused at the top of one the side trails and pulled out his water bottle. He sat down to take a drink and was startled when he looked up to see an elderly man standing on the trail just below him. He realized that he had seen the man once before, sitting in the Thurston Hotel gardens, the night he'd heard Nora singing in the gazebo. The old man was even dressed in the same clothes - a blue suit jacket, dress pants and a blue plaid shirt open at the neck. Hardly the clothes he would need for a walk in the woods, Jim thought.

"Are you helping with the search?" Jim called out as he stood up.

The man silently shook his head. He pointed down the trail, and beckoned Jim to follow him. *Weird*, thought Jim.

"Are you okay?" he asked. The man nodded and continued down the trail. *Maybe he'd found something.* Jim followed behind him. Just before they reached the picnic site, the man picked up a stick and scratched something into the dirt on the trail. Jim walked up and looked at it. It was the letter "N" and the letter "G"

"Nora? Glenna? Do you know where they are? Tell me!"

The man smiled and nodded, pointing in the direction of town.

"They're in Harmony?" Jim asked. The man nodded.

"Why won't you talk to me? What happened to them?" Jim looked back down at the letters in the dirt. When he looked up, the man had vanished.

Where did he go? Jim stood in confusion for a few minutes, then ran up the trail to the picnic site. Nick greeted him.

"No sign yet, Jim," he said apologetically. "Sorry. I gave Henry some food and water."

"Thanks. Nick, I need to drive to town, right now. Tell the wardens if you see them."

Nick nodded. Jim unleashed Henry from the tree, loaded him in the truck and drove off at top speed.

CHAPTER EIGHTEEN

Arthur pulled his car up in front of the RCMP post in Harmony. Nora jumped out and ran to the door. It was locked. She rang the bell. No answer.

"They must have left already," Flora said.

Nora stood for a minute, thinking. "Let's try Jim's house," she said, and gave Arthur the directions. When they arrived at the house, Glenna ran inside.

"Dad! Daddy!" she called. No answer. She ran back to the car. "He's not there," she said.

"We'd better head back downtown," Nora said. "Somewhere central, like the Thurston Hotel. It's right in the middle of Main Street. Someone might know what's going on."

Arthur drove to the hotel. Mrs. Arbuckle was standing in front, holding Betty Jo in her arms. They got out of the car.

"Nora! Glenna! My God, where have you been? Jim has been looking for you, and so have the Mounties! We've all been worried sick!"

She handed Betty Jo to Flora, hugged both Nora and Glenna and then turned back to the Gibsons.

"Thank you for bringing them home." She shook their hands warmly before retrieving Betty Jo. "I'll see that Jim and the police are notified. Now you'd better come in and have some tea. That's the best thing for all of us right now."

Arthur Gibson looked down at his striped pajamas and bare feet, then looked over at his wife in her robe and curlers. "Sounds good," he said.

Just as they were turning to go into the hotel, they heard a horn honking. Nora recognized Jim's truck speeding down Main Street. Glenna shouted and ran out to the curb. Minutes later, she was in her father's arms.

Jim held her tightly. "Glenna, I've been so worried. Where did you get to? Thank God you're safe."

"Daddy...Daddy...You're squeezing me so tight I can't breathe!" Jim released her and took her face in his hands. "Don't ever, ever, do that again."

"Dad. I didn't...she took me. And she took Nora."

"Who did?"

"My mother."

Jim looked up with dismay at Nora who nodded. He released Glenna and walked toward her. She thought he would ask for an explanation but instead he crushed her in his arms. "Nora, I'm so sorry. I should never have left you."

Nora stroked his hair. "Jim, it's all over. Glenna is safe, and so am I. But Rachelle is still out there. I've let the Mounties know."

"What did she do to you?" Jim asked.

Mrs. Arbuckle stepped in. "Just a minute, Jim. As I said, we all need to sit down and have some tea. Nora, you can explain what happened, but I think Glenna needs some rest right now. Jim, take her up to my suite and have her lie down. I'll send up some sweet tea for her. Henry can stay in the truck for now. The rest of us will be in the Margaret Library."

In the hotel, Jim took Mrs. Arbuckle's key card, put his arm around Glenna and walked with her to the elevator. Mrs. Arbuckle led Nora and the Gibsons to the library, asked the staff to notify the police and requested that they not be disturbed by other guests. Then she ordered tea and sandwiches for everyone.

* * *

Glenna washed her face as Jim turned down the covers on the bed. He helped Glenna remove her shoes and outer clothes and then tucked her in, sitting on the bed beside her.

Glenna was shaking. He wrapped a warm throw around her shoulders. He was relieved to see Poppy arrive with a tray containing hot tea and sandwiches.

"Poor love," Poppy cooed, patting Glenna's hand.

"Thank you," Jim said.

After Poppy had gone, Glenna sipped some tea and ate a sandwich, then related what had happened.

"Nora was so brave, Daddy. She smashed a bottle and cut us free. If it wasn't for her we'd still be there."

Jim stroked her hair. "No need to explain everything now, Sweetheart. Nora will tell me the details. You're safe. I'm here. Just get some sleep."

"I love you, Daddy."

"I love you so much, Sprout. Everything's going to be all right. She's not going to hurt you anymore. Sleep now."

Glenna closed her eyes and was asleep in minutes.

Jim quietly closed the door before making his way down to the library. When he reached the lobby, the staff told him there was a phone call for him at the reception desk.

* * *

"Thank you so much, Mrs. Arbuckle," Nora said, grateful to eat something. It seemed days since the picnic. Was it just yesterday? How could all this have happened in just twenty-four hours? Finishing her third cup of strong, sweet tea, she was happy to see Jim returning.

"Glenna's sleeping," he said. "I've just been talking to the Mounties."

He sat down beside Nora on the red brocade loveseat and took her hand.

"Now tell us," he said.

Nora told her story slowly. She paused a few times as emotion overcame her. Finally, she had related everything. "And then we came here," she finished.

Putting her head on Jim's shoulder, she began to shake and for the first time, she allowed all the pent-up emotion to be released. Jim held her close while she cried it out.

Mrs. Arbuckle and the Gibsons sat silently, absorbing the story they had just been told.

"What you did was so courageous, Nora. I can't believe this happened," Mrs. Arbuckle remarked. "What kind of person would do this to their own daughter?"

"She won't be hurting anyone else, ever again." Jim said.

Nora sat up. "What do you mean?" she asked.

Jim looked around at all of them.

"Rachelle's dead."

No one spoke for several minutes.

"Jim, I'm sorry," Nora said.

"I'm fine, Nora. I thought it could come to this someday, I just didn't know when."

Jim shared the conversation he had had with the Mounties. "She managed to wound one of the officers, but thank God she didn't kill anyone. They had no choice but to defend themselves. The paramedics took the boy and the Mountie who was shot to the hospital. They found a ransom note for Nora and Glenna in Rachelle's coat pocket."

Jim looked down. "I can't help feeling I could have prevented this. I knew what Rachelle was capable of…I should have warned the police as soon as she came to town. Glenna and Nora could have been spared this trauma…"

"No, Jim." Nora's voice was firm. "No one could have predicted she'd go so far. You did your best to protect Glenna…and me. Don't let yourself think that way. We're here and we're safe."

"That's right, dear," Mrs. Arbuckle weighed in. "Now you need to get on with your life."

Jim turned to Nora. "It was that man on the trail that let me know you were back in town."

"What man?" Nora asked.

"That elderly man I saw sitting in the hotel gardens, the night we met in the gazebo," Jim replied. "He must have come to help us search. I met him on a side trail and he beckoned me to follow him. But he never said a word. Finally, he just scratched your initials in the dirt with a stick and then pointed back to Harmony. Somehow I knew what he meant, that I had to get back to town. Then he just disappeared."

Nora and Mrs. Arbuckle spoke at the same time.

"Mr. A!"

"Walter!"

Jim saw the two women exchange smiles.

"Who?" he asked.

"I'm afraid you've seen a ghost, Jim." Nora whispered.

"What?" Jim looked at her incredulously.

Mrs. Arbuckle smiled. "Now you're really part of Harmony, young man. My dear departed husband, Walter, has contacted many of the people in this town. You're just the latest."

Jim shook his head. "A ghost? I don't believe in ghosts!"

Nora laughed. "Whether or not you do, you've met one, Jim Barnes! Better just accept it."

Jim grinned. "If he helped get my girls back to me, then I'll believe in him gladly and with heartfelt thanks!" He leaned over and kissed Nora.

"Bravo!" said Mrs. Arbuckle.

"Arthur, drink up your tea!" said Flora, adjusting her robe and for the first time noticing her husband's disheveled hair and unshaven face. "We still haven't checked out of our motel room."

CHAPTER NINETEEN

A week later, Jim sat across from Nora for their second dinner together in the Foothills Dining Room. They held hands over the table.

"Nora, I still haven't thanked you for saving Glenna." Jim leaned toward her. "I can't imagine what would have happened if Rachelle had come back while you were trying to get free. I've had nightmares about it."

"Those bad dreams will go away, Jim. All that matters is that Glenna is safe and Rachelle is gone. She won't ever interfere with you and Glenna again."

Jim brought her hand up and kissed her open palm. "Thanks to you and thanks to Mr. Arbuckle," he said. "I have my daughter back."

"And what a wonderful daughter you have, Jim. She was very brave and kept her cool, even though she was frightened. You should be proud."

"I am, and I'm proud of you, too. When I said you were the best thing that had happened to me in years, I meant it."

Nora blushed.

"What do you say we take a stroll around the gardens?" Jim suggested.

As they stepped outside, they spied a figure sitting on a bench across the lawn.

"It's him!" Jim said, watching with astonishment as Walter Arbuckle waved at them. A moment later, he had vanished. Jim looked at Nora and she leaned her head on his shoulder, smiling up at him.

"See?" she said.

"I guess I better start believing in ghosts and give you a lot more respect for your psychic abilities," Jim said, "There are more things in heaven and earth…!"

"…than are dreamt of in your philosophy. Shakespeare, right?" Nora finished.

He took her hand and led her toward the gazebo. They sat quietly, looking up at the stars.

He drew Nora close and kissed her. "You are the woman I've been waiting for, Nora Fitzgerald. When I realized you were in danger I couldn't bear the thought of losing you."

Nora took his face in her hands. "You and Glenna mean the world to me, Jim. You've both given me so much happiness. My one thought when Glenna and I were hostages was how to get both of us safely back to Harmony…and to you."

Jim leaned forward and kissed her again. Then he stood up and sank down on one knee in front of her. He pulled a small box out of his pocket, and opened it to reveal a sparkling diamond, set in a silver band with a Celtic interlace design. Nora gasped.

"I love you, Nora Fitzgerald. Glenna and I both love you. Now that you've saved her, will you save me too? Will you marry me, Nora?"

"I will," said Nora, tears filling her eyes.

EPILOGUE

Glenna laughed out loud as she watched Henry chase his tail in the hotel gardens. He looked even funnier with that big white bow tied around his neck. Henry was dressed in his wedding finery, just as she was. Glenna looked down at her lacy blue dress and matching shoes and a wave of joy flowed through her. *It's the best day of my life*, she thought, looking over toward the large white tent set up near the decorated gazebo. She could see her father and her new mother sharing a kiss as the wedding guests applauded. Mrs. Arbuckle was making a toast with a glass of champagne. Night was falling. Soon the music would start and everyone would be on the dance floor. Nick had promised to dance with her, a fact which made Glenna's heart beat faster every time she thought about it. She looked back at Henry, who was now standing still looking at something, his tail wagging. Glenna followed his gaze and saw an elderly man standing nearby. The man had a jolly face and winked at Glenna. She winked back. He pointed upward and Glenna could see that the moon was rising and the stars were coming out, one by one. When she looked down again the man had vanished. *That's funny. Where did he go?* Glenna called to Henry and ran back to the tent where her parents were waiting for her with open arms.

BOOKS IN THE THURSTON HOTEL SERIES

The Thurston Heirloom, Book 9
By Suzanne Stengl

An Angel's Secret, Book 10
By Ellen Jorgy

To a Tea, Book 11
By Katie O'Connor

A Thurston Christmas, Book 12
By Brenda Sinclair

ABOUT THE AUTHOR

Maeve Buchanan grew up on the Canadian prairies in a family who loved books. As a girl, she spent much of her time reading and dreaming up stories, often illustrating the stories as she went.

As an adult, Maeve studied at the Alberta College of Art and Design and then worked at a wide variety of jobs, including graphic arts, building playgrounds in the Arctic, working as an historical interpreter and managing marketing for a major bookstore chain.

Maeve completed a degree in English Literature and Medieval Studies at the University of Victoria. This was followed by three years of medieval manuscript research at the University of Glasgow, Scotland and extensive travelling throughout the British Isles.

Returning to Canada from Britain, Maeve came back to her prairie roots by settling in Edmonton, Alberta.

After joining the Romance Writers of America (Calgary chapter), Maeve's literary talents found a new home in the Romance genre, and she hasn't looked back since!

Maeve's current work, ***The Starlight Garden*** is an adult contemporary romance set in the Canadian Rockies. She is currently working on another adult contemporary romance and planning future books set in the regency and medieval periods.

Travelling is one of Maeve's passions. She has travelled widely in Canada and Britain as well as spending time in Paris and her favorite getaway, the Island of Maui in Hawaii.

You can find Maeve Buchanan at:

Website: www.maevebuchanan.com

Email: maeve@maevebuchanan.com

FB: www.facebook.com/maevebuchananauthor